The Plea

Previous Books Published

Below are other books in the Joe Kavinsky mystery/detective series by John St. Robert, the pen name for former police reporter John Simplot.

Going Down—Hailed as a "thriller" that has won top reviews and broad readership. As the first novel in this series, it focuses on identical twin sisters, one honest and the other deceptive, and a fitness center that's really a drug hangout.
Some reviews:

> *"Would make a very good movie—great drama, clever plot and ending"*
>
> —Boise, Idaho lawyer
>
> *"Keeps you reading and you don't want to put it down"*
>
> —St. Paul art director

Tune of Terror—A follow-up tale of harmonious action, adventure and intrigue with some Mideast opium mixed in. Local and federal authorities team up to capture the clever drug lord and gang at the Mall of America where a pianist helps capture the terrorists with special music. A fraudulent DNA exam at a major clinic and surprising recovery of money also provide elements for an unusual plot twist.

> *"Has all the earmarks of a fiction thriller classic"*
>
> —Editor, Chicago celebrity newsletter
>
> *"The detective and his reporter uncle make a great team in fighting crime that otherwise would remain undercover"*
>
> —St. Paul meeting planner and writer

THE PLEA

John St. Robert

iUniverse, Inc.
New York Lincoln Shanghai

The Plea

All Rights Reserved © 2004 by John Simplot

No part of this book may be reproduced or transmitted in any form or by any means, graphic, electronic, or mechanical, including photocopying, recording, taping, or by any information storage retrieval system, without the written permission of the publisher.

iUniverse, Inc.

For information address:
iUniverse, Inc.
2021 Pine Lake Road, Suite 100
Lincoln, NE 68512
www.iuniverse.com

ISBN: 0-595-30737-X

Printed in the United States of America

Acknowledgements

Many thanks to those who contributed information and advice for this story. Special appreciation is due to my legal advisor who reviewed the story so it is plausible from the standpoint of the judicial process, and to those friends who offered advice on style and descriptions befitting the characters portrayed in this timely and sensitive fictional tale. My gratitude also is due to veteran writer Harry Clark and to Janet Winsand, academic computer consultant of the College of St. Catherine in the Twin Cities who helped to keep my computer going.

Prologue

Although running can be healthy, it can also be dangerous if it leads to trouble. Joe Kavinsky has been running every which way—or so it seems. One way has already led to the capture of a gang of terrorists at a giant shopping mall. The other is directed at protecting a pretty Muslim woman accused of being a gang member...but Joe knows in his heart she's innocent and helped to catch the terrorists.

    Nearly out of breath from his many fast-paced duties as a local police detective and undercover DEA agent, Joe stops at times to realize that much of his running about began when he fell in love and married a daughter of a lawyer profiting from drug smuggling. Her father committed suicide to escape arrest by leaping off a ship near Bermuda where Joe and his bride were on their honeymoon. His wife was found innocent of her father's wrongdoings, but her twin sister was implicated and awaits trial. Happiness surfaces, however, when the father left his daughters millions of dollars as an inheritance, minus all the "dirty drug money" that sank with him in the ocean.

    To add to Joe's pressures, he is determined to find the killer of his police partner who was mysteriously murdered while jailed for being part of the drug dealing in Bermuda—where an ex police chief and coroner in Joe's home town were caught trying to fish out the money that fell into the ocean. How is Joe able to catch up on all this? Realizing he desperately needs help, but must be extremely careful not to rush to justice, he once again turns to his DEA pal and, of course, to his always reliable and greatly experienced police reporter buddy—his uncle Al.

CHAPTER 1

The tiny cell was dark and damp. The small frail woman sitting in a corner could barely be seen. Her face was still hidden by a veil and her body covered by a Muslim robe. She had no visitors, and none were welcomed judging from the piles of junk near the entrance to her cell. There was even a garbage can intentionally put next to the bars by the U.S. marshal guarding her. The whole scene stunk to high hell, thought detective Joe Kavinsky as he approached the silent cloaked prisoner.

Upset, he almost stumbled on the cluttered narrow stairway leading to where she was being held…on charges yet to be filed. He cursed to himself, irritated at why this young lady with her head down, seemingly in despair, was being treated so shabbily after helping both federal and local authorities capture a group of terrorists planning an attack on Minnesota's gigantic shopping mall.

To add to his anger, Joe was rudely stopped by the female deputy marshal who insisted on closely studying his credentials. She seemed to take unnecessary time noting nearly every item in his pockets qualifying him to be in this gloomy "hole" in the basement of a nearby Twin Cities' suburban Post Office building. Many on the main floor of the building, although somewhat attractive on the outside, were probably completely unaware that such a frightening federal detention center existed beneath them as they purchased stamps and did their mailing.

Joe was commanded to keep his visit brief. He barely had time to remind the indifferent jailer that the person behind bars should be treated better; that a terrible mistake was being made by what he considered illegal confinement and that she should be quickly released. Upon entering the filthy 8x8ft. cell, crowded by a toilet with very little privacy and a leaky sink, hard cot and soiled mattress, it was hard to talk since the deputy turned a nearby radio on so loudly. The weeping prisoner could only nod to let Joe know she could hear him as he sat on the cot holding her hands to show support.

The buxom guard didn't bother to have him sign out but stared at him with her fists clenched. Unable to restrain her thoughts any longer, she said with a scowl as he departed:

"Why the hell are you visiting such crap? She was going to do us all in."

Joe didn't waste time to respond, or dignify the question. As usual, he was in a hurry to cope with his own duties, as a detective in the Minneapolis police department and undercover agent for the Drug Enforcement Agency (DEA), a job he was selected for by helping to catch drug smugglers operating within the Twin Cities and islands of Bermuda and Bahamas. On his way back to his precinct, he realized his attempts at consoling the distraught jailed lady were futile. By the way she was being treated who could blame her for already being suspicious of authorities who apparently didn't live up to granting her what she was promised, Joe thought.

CHAPTER 2

The disgusted detective became further upset upon his return to his desk at the police station. In fact, he felt he could use some consoling himself after his boss, Police Chief Fred Hermes, dropped an ugly slightly used knife with a long blade on his desk.

He could only stare at the knife in virtual disbelief since it reportedly was used to kill his partner, Dave Paulson. He was notified recently that Paulson was found stabbed to death in a Bermuda jail after admitting being involved in the terrorist plot at the giant Twin Cities area mall. The knife, sealed in a clear plastic envelope, was still stained with blood, a grim reminder of Joe's recent Bermuda trip to bring Dave's body back home. A note was attached from the DNA lab confirming that this indeed was the death weapon.

At first, authorities believed Dave had committed suicide by stabbing himself to escape disgrace and punishment for conspiring with international drug lords. His bleeding body was found lying on a cot inside a desolate unkempt cell in the bowels of a sleazy jail on the outskirts of Hamilton, the Bermuda capital. Paulson was being held there for further interrogation by both Bermuda and U.S. officials. Joe visited him in jail just before his death to learn more why his fellow cop was helping the drug smugglers. Forensic experts at police headquarters, where Joe was stationed as well as Paulson, reported that the fatal wound in the middle of Paulson's back could not possibly be self inflicted. Prints on the knife, returned on a plane carrying Paulson's remains, were not the victim's…leaving Joe with the question: then whose prints were they?

"The sample of blood on the blade is Dave's—but the finger prints aren't," explained the DNA researcher, who concurred with forensic associates that it would be physically impossible for Paulson to stab himself so deeply in the middle of his back.

Joe theorized that someone in Bermuda wanted to shut Paulson up permanently since he knew too much about the illegal drug business going on involving the Twin Cities and Bermuda. After all, Bermuda and the Bahamas were both considered ideal havens to hide ill-gotten money, he realized. Joe also knew a lot about those islands, where he discovered lots of drug smuggling between there and the U.S. heartland. As a veteran cop, he was used to seeing everyone from misguided teenagers to hard-boiled thugs and smooth-talking corporate executives behind bars on drug charges. But not cops. He knew Paulson may have had this coming and certainly betrayed his police oath.

Most of those behind bars accused of drug dealing or terrorism, he realized, deserved to be locked up. However, he couldn't help but think that one who certainly shouldn't be receiving harsh treatment was that very attractive veiled young lady being detained in that gosh-awful cell in the pit of the federal building.

Indeed, local authorities as well as the DEA and other feds were indebted to her for assisting with rounding up drug terrorists descending on Minnesota. Although her name was Salid Ashid, authorities preferred to simply call her Sally. This was also more in keeping with her captivating looks, which seemed to warm up the cold atmosphere of the jail where she was to stay until her arraignment. It was very apparent that she was trying to be as cooperative as possible under such conditions and wanted very much to help authorities to bring her many former drug acquaintances to justice. Unfortunately, one of those "acquaintances" sadly enough was Paulson.

The ringing of his desk phone interrupted Joe's thoughts about the knife, which he was told by the chief to keep as evidence. He quickly put it back in a drawer before responding to the caller. It was his wife, Sarah, updating him on some more bad news—which he certainly didn't need at this time.

"Joe, the marshal's office called. They want you down at the detention center as soon as you can get there. That girl you talked to is trying to commit suicide," his wife warned. Kavinsky wasn't too surprised. The disgusting environment surrounding this mysterious young lady from the Mideast, and her sudden complete isolation from friends, and mistrust in most everyone she had trusted, were surely creating a desire for her to end her life, he reasoned.

He realized this wasn't just any prisoner. After all, he was present when she received the promise from authorities to be considered for a plea bargain by leading them to those intent on terror. In his opinion, to treat her also as a terrorist by reneging on a written agreement for amnesty made the captors far more untrusting than the prisoner.

He kept this in mind upon rushing back again to the forlorn cell of the seemingly bewildered and frightened girl. He hadn't seen her much without a scarf hiding most of her face, following the custom of the religion and Afghanistan area she represented. When he did, it was like the unveiling of beauty—even more than he had imagined.

Before receiving permission to talk with her, however, the chief marshal now on duty described the scene he encountered earlier that day. Upon delivering her breakfast, he noticed that she had tied her facial scarf around her neck onto a post and was standing on the cot in the cell ready to jump off and be strangled, he reported.

"Why in hell would you leave her unnoticed?" interrupted Joe, upset over the apparent negligent way she was being detained.

"She said it was important to her to keep her scarf as a token of her faith. We were just trying to do what she wanted," explained the jailer in defense. Cooling off somewhat, Kavinsky pointed a finger at the guy in charge while reminding him once again that Salid is to be given preferential treatment and not be considered guilty of anything until a proper hearing is concluded, charges if any are filed, and only after an impartial trial, if necessary, decides her degree of guilt. In fact, he added, she should be regarded more as a loyal friend of the nation at this point.

With that, the marshal looked at his associates, grinning as though Kavinsky was nuts. "A friend—how can you say that? She was with those evil people at our mall and clinic who were all set to blow these places up."

"It didn't happen, did it?" noted Joe looking sternly at the marshal. "And it didn't—because of this young lady's help."

Listening to all this near her cell, Salid was finally smiling and nodding as though agreeing with Joe's comments. She almost seemed on the verge of applauding when he completed his case by saying: "You must show her the respect and thanks we owe her for tipping us off to catch those guys—at the risk of being horribly mutilated or killed." The marshal also nodded at this, apparently accepting Kavinsky's viewpoint and even grinnng at his prisoner to give her assurance of improved treatment.

"We'll keep a much better eye on her Joe. I know we owe her thanks. I wish we had a better place than this, but the finances for our detention sites are at a minimum, like everything else on the federal budget these days."

As Joe departed, after waving farewell to Salid, the marshal winked and tugged his arm whispering teasingly, "I might add, she's a pretty one to keep an eye on."

When Joe arrived home that evening, he chatted with his wife about Salid's situation, although being careful not to mention the attractiveness of the jailed woman. Sarah was still slightly upset over all the phone calls Salid had made to Joe before being jailed keeping him secretly informed about the status of the terrorists she was with. It was obvious that Sarah was still wondering about the attention given to her husband by this comely miss. Despite realizing this was all part of police strategy, she wasn't sure if some of those calls weren't primarily to chat with her handsome husband.

"I remember that cute little gal," said Sarah without much fear of any competition. Indeed, Sarah, 26, had been a beauty queen in college where she also won scholastic honors while meeting Joe at the Prom. However, both their minds turned quickly on the cheerfulness of home when their baby daughter, Matilda, began dropping toys from her high chair. When trying teasingly to get her talkative parents to pick them up, both began thinking about family happiness, which also helped to remind them of the loneliness of the jailed woman—who may also have a family somewhere.

"How can we find out?" asked Sarah while rocking the baby. "After all, my sister Susan wasn't detained long and she seemed to be treated okay." This reminded Joe that his wife's twin sister is now in a very first-class detention center with some of the comforts of home while awaiting trial on charges of helping her mobster boyfriend conduct terrorism in and around the Twin Cities. Sarah also wondered if her sister was being given special privileges by being the daughter of a former affluent lawyer, although Sarah was greatly embarrassed by the wrongdoings of her sister.

The only thing Sarah shared now with Susan was the considerable money she and her sister both inherited from their father who was tied in with drug terrorists before his death. Joe often wondered why he was even working with the money they now have. "But when you're a cop, you don't stop," he used as his motto and inspiration.

To Sarah's question about Salid, Joe replied, "I'm not sure how to help her through this, honey. But we might, if we could find out more about her home life: like where is she from? are her parents still living? and how did she get involved with those evil guys in the first place? You know—the kind of personal things that'll help us relate more with her...to let her know we care, and where she's coming from." Sarah added, "Yes—and if she has any family here or nearby who could give her comfort."

Surprisingly, however, even before he could begin digging into Salid's background, Joe was given unexpected help the next day when the head marshal called.

"Just thought you'd like to know your little gal Sal is not alone down here anymore."

"What do you mean? There's hardly room for her in that cell as it is."

"There is now. She has a visitor sitting with her."

"Must be a lawyer—I didn't think she had any friends around here. I understood she was all alone in this country…if she had any family they're probably still in that desolate, impoverished part of the world where she's from," Joe said with a shrug.

"I don't know anything about that Joe. The visitor's a woman and I'm not sure if she's a lawyer. But she did have proper authorization to be admitted. I'd say she's more a pro-activist than a legal aid." The chief marshal added with a chuckle, "but she's a cutie, too—I think you should come down here to meet her. And, by the way, she's also making a big fuss over why and how Salid is being held. Which is why I'm calling."

Joe pondered this for a few minutes and then set aside his work load piling up at the precinct. He straightened his tie, glanced in the mirror to see if his hair looked okay, and then rushed off through the heart of town to the outlying detention center.

But, alas, by the time he arrived, the mysterious visitor had departed, despite all the attempts the marshal claimed he made to detain her until Joe arrived.

The marshal explained, "I tried to keep that visitor here until you came, but she said she was in a hurry. I still don't know what she does—and she wouldn't say anything about herself. In fact, she and Salid almost spoke in a whisper."

While the marshal was talking, Kavinsky was checking out the list of visitors to the jail in the past few days. The guest book was very sparse. The last name on it was so poorly scribbled that it was unreadable. He realized, however, that it actually takes a U.S. federal attorney to instruct the marshal about who may visit her.

Joe turned to look at Salid who was staring at him by now behind her bars. He could feel the intensity of her gaze—as if trying to engulf his soul, scolding him for keeping her locked up. It made him feel he was really the one who was guilty, by not living up to giving her the freedom she expected. It was as if her eyes were telling him he was ignoring that authorities cut a deal and changed their minds.

For a moment, Kavinsky hesitated to return her look. He was determined to do his part in upholding this so-called plea bargain, but realized it also involved help and cooperation from others who, at least for now, seemed reluctant. What added to this unfairness, thought Joe, was that some authorities involved also agreed to a plea of three Mideast researchers at the state's major clinic who were accused of concealing DNA results implicating the terrorist leader. He figured, apparently they were so important to the clinic they were able to diplomatically get amnesty quickly and without detention.

With all this in mind, he walked to her cell and beckoned the marshal to open it for him. But when he entered, she suddenly turned her back on him.

"Guess I deserve that, as well as my police chief and DEA buddy who witnessed your plea and acknowledged it," remarked Joe responding to her body language. "I haven't forgotten you Sal, nor, I'm sure, have the others. It takes time—like reminders to the proper officials that you're due for a very fair hearing."

Turning to look at Joe again, she said, as though pouting like a child, "I am innocent in all this—and should be treated as such. My husband, Amad, deceived me saying he was an honorable lawman and needed me to help arrest the terrorist leader."

She cried, "I love America—I didn't want anyone to hurt it like the leader planned. My plea to all of this is…I'm simply not guilty!"

Kavinsky seemed startled on hearing the word husband. He had no idea she was more than just a lover of Amad, who pretended to be a detective helping Joe and Paulson catch terrorist suspects involved with the leader's descent on Minnesota. When the so-called leader, Robert Beck, questioned Amad's loyalty, he killed him.

"I was with you, your police chief and federal officer when Amad and I agreed to spy on Beck and lead you to him in return for our plea," she reminded Joe.

"Yes—and I assure you I'm doing everything possible in seeing that you get it. I'm deeply sorry about Amad. I'm very surprised he was your husband, however, and know you also were putting yourself into great harm's way trying to assist us."

With that, she turned completely to face the detective and finally smiled somewhat. "I thank you for that Mr. Kavinsky I don't have many friends here, and those I have I must sincerely trust."

"I realize that Salid. And please believe me when I say I'm your friend and you can trust me."

He then added, "By the way, who came to visit you most recently? she seemed to also be a friend I'm told."

"She's more than that…she is my sister."

"Your sister—but I understood you had no relatives around this country."

"She's not from here—she is a former resident of Afghanistan." Sensing Joe's bewilderment over this, Salid explained, "She belongs to an international group of Christian missionaries who are allowed to help those in need—wherever that may be around the world."

"And in this case, that happens to be right here—is that correct Salid?" concluded Joe.

"Yes, she heard I was in need and found me here."

"But she's a Christian—and you…you're a Muslim—right?"

"That is also correct—but we both believe in a just and merciful God."

"And you hope we do too…isn't that also right?" asked Joe assuming what Salid was thinking.

At this, Salid stepped closer to Kavinsky and smiled. "I know you do detective. And I am now certain you will treat me fairly. I can tell by the way you are fighting for this. It is the others I am afraid of."

"You mean our judges?"

"Yes—but also the judges in my country, the ones they call the Taliban."

"Well, you don't have to worry about that—we'll protect you from them. I'm almost certain you won't have to go back to them."

"But you can't. They will either persecute and kill me in this country or wait until I return to mine to do so," she said desperately.

Considering all this, Joe wondered out loud, "Did your sister mention anything about this?"

"Yes—she, too, knows how vicious the Taliban can be. They are furious even now that I have sided in with you and other authorities of your nation and will use me as an example of what happens to those who betray them.

"Especially any woman who may be so bold to do so," Salid added.

Joe simply nodded his head, acknowledging he was aware of how women are treated by such stern Islamic fundamentalists—and knowing that it seemed nearly impossible to prevent such cruelty.

Realizing retaliation was probably in the minds and hearts of those already angered that one of their own woman abused their conservative rules, Kavinsky sat down on the cot with Salid and focused on how to prevent such vengeance happening to her.

"We'll try to find you the very best legal counsel there is, Sal. Especially one who knows your background. But this must be authorized by the attorney general."

Salid raised her hand to make a point. "But in some parts of my country anyone who is a drug suspect is considered filth. They can expect only flowers, a minimum of legal help, and can only briefly communicate with family and friends."

He emphasized, "But you're in this country now. Believe me, the chief of police, the DEA, and, of course, myself will all vouch for your fine help in preventing terrorism. We were all there when the plea bargain was discussed."

"Yes, and Amad and your partner Paulson also were there—but they are dead now. Both murdered."

"And the man who killed Amad is also behind bars. There is no chance that he will ever be freed. We know he threatened you and made you cooperate at gunpoint," Kavinsky added.

He then got up from the cot, placed his hand on his chin as though in deep thought and noted, "But we still don't know who murdered Paulson, my partner. It must have been someone who urgently wanted him silenced." Salid commented, "and he cannot help me now either. Do you suppose the Taliban got to him?"

"Not likely," replied Joe. "They're a bit off their turf in Bermuda. But come to think of it—they are in this country, too."

Joe suddenly snapped his fingers and emphasized, "That's why it's most crucial that the very best attorney is chosen. One that's picked with care...one that can relate to this—or at least keep an open mind to what's been happening."

On considering this further he noted, "However, I have nothing to say about who that may be. A federal district judge of Minnesota will be involved in this."

He added, "hell, for that matter no charges have been filed against you yet—nor should there be. And how can they still be holding you here?"

Joe turned to look at the marshal, saying: "She can't be detained here very long—a few more days and she should be given her hearing promptly when a defense attorney is assigned by the court to her case. Isn't that right marshal?"

"Joe, I'm not the guy in charge here. But I believe you're right. This is just a temporary detention site. She could very well be freed tomorrow, for all I know."

"Good, but until then I want her to be given the very best treatment. And if there are any problems let me know immediately."

With that, Kavinsky squeezed Salid's hand in support, as she clenched onto a cell bar with the other, emphasizing that she's in good hands and need not fear.

Before leaving, however, Kavinsky remembered one other matter. "By the way, where and how can I contact your sister?"

"She goes by the name of Paola Murka. She told me she stays with a group of other sisters in a small cottage on the outskirts of North St. Paul. She left me no phone numbers or any other information regarding her home."

"That's okay. I'll find a way to reach her."

"But why would you want to?" asked Salid.

"Who knows—she also may be able to help us help you," explained Joe. "What order does she belong to?"

"It's with the Byzantines, but I don't know their official name. I am with the church of Allah, as you know." She added, "although we both had the same mother, we did not have the same father. Mine was strict and whipped us if we strayed away from our fundamental Muslim faith. Paola's father was also a holy man who left his family to become a missionary in the mountains of Afghanistan."

"What became of him?"

"He was horribly killed by a group of fundamentalists who caught him befriending a Muslim girl."

"Were they the Talibans?"

"I believe they were. That's when I escaped and fled to join up with the followers of my native faith in America. But some were with the Beck group."

"Did you know they were terrorists?"

"No, never. I was able to come to this country with my husband who had a student visa, although I have no citizen papers. Amad misled me into thinking his group was holy and deserving of much loyalty and service in the name of Allah."

"And that's when you joined them—not knowing their terrorist or drug smuggling plans?"

"Yes, yes...ask Paola, she knows about this."

Upon assuring Salid that he would check into this, and letting the marshal know that the next visitor to talk to her may be a U.S. attorney, he left by warning him sarcastically, "You'd better get this place looking better—or they may be charging you guys for woman abuse." On arriving back at his precinct, he began looking up Paola's address. However, there was no Murka listed in the phone book. Knowing that Byzantine is a Greek Christian rite, he tried contacting the local chancery office for information.

Before reaching for his phone, however, a call came in from his DEA pal Terry Johnson, an energetic "drug buster" slightly older than 35-year-old Kavinsky. "Joe, the U.S. marshal just told me you're checking on our Muslim gal Sal. Don't get too impatient, I'm told a lawyer well acquainted with Mideast law, protocol and all that stuff will visit her in the next few days. You should also know the FBI has entered into this."

"The next few days, Terry?" echoed Joe. "Hell, you and I know she shouldn't be there to begin with. I can't help but think we're violating a trust—we offered her a plea bargain in return for her help. She stuck her neck out for us at and could have been tortured or even murdered."

"I know, I know...but we still have to follow official procedure. If we violate this, even our president may be down on us."

"Yes, but if she isn't defended properly, she could get back into the hands of the terrorists—and God knows what will happen to her then." warned Kavinsky. "If she isn't charged for anything soon she should be let go, I repeat, we have no right at all to hold her forever."

CHAPTER 3

"I know how you feel," responded Johnson to Joe's plea for Salid's freedom. "But you must know that our nation is uptight these days over all the trickery and terrorist schemes to bring us down. The approach by all those in charge of homeland security is to make sure everything is investigated thoroughly before making any decisions. If the Justice Department claims she's a terrorist she can be deported right away by the INS." He added, "no doubt about it—she needs a great attorney."

"So who is this 'super attorney'?"

"You know as much as I do. Where he's coming from, or the exact time is still a mystery to me. But as soon as I find out you'll be among the first to know," assured Johnson. "For that matter, I don't know if this person will be a he or a she."

"Well, if it takes much longer I'm going to let my reporter uncle, Al Benjamin, know," warned Joe. "He'll recall how helpful Salid was to all of us. Our mega mall and clinic may not even be standing if it wasn't for her. What a story that'll make for his paper."

"Don't threaten me, Joe. I'm completely on your side. Guess we'll just have to wait to see that so-called 'super guy' at the preliminary hearing. You know yourself that we have to handle this with kid gloves. For that matter, the Council on America Islamic Relations may already be filing a complaint against us."

Johnson continued, "hell, many are probably viewing every Islamic community in this country with suspicion. This is especially so now that our country should be focusing more on terrorism cases, including developing undercover informants, and less on other ordinary type cases."

With that, Kavinsky sat back in his office chair and lit another cigarette. After blowing out smoke, he saw the knife again on his desk, also seemingly waiting for some answers. Although the blood on it was dark now from the time of the killing it still reminded the detective that someone was getting away with murder. He tried recalling everything he could think of leading up to Paulson's death, but nothing stood out pointing to anyone who possibly may be the murderer.

However, maybe…just maybe, he thought, Bermuda officials could have some answers by now. But, then again, who should he check with? About the only one he knew probably still in Bermuda was the DEA agent assigned by the feds to also help investigate the charge that Paulson was involved with drug smuggling and laundering on that island. This agent was traveling incognito, Joe was told, probably on the same plane he was on.

But who was the agent? Joe pondered this for awhile until being interrupted again by a call from Johnson.

"Joe, I think we've traced down Sal's sister…or should I say the sister who is a sister of that gal in detention. In any case, she's at the Byzantine convent house at 1560 Howard Street." Terry could be heard chuckling over his attempt at being funny.

"Great, I'll call on her to get more information on that 'super attorney'."

"Yeah, she even has an unlisted phone number."

Just as Joe was about to hang up, he remembered to ask about the DNA agent with him in Bermuda who may know more about Paulson's death.

"Who the hell was that guy? I was so preoccupied thinking about Paulson that I forgot his name," he muttered to Terry.

"Her name, Joe, her name!" urged Johnson. "Remember, he's a she."

"Really—I didn't even check this out. That's not like me, guess I was too absorbed in thinking about poor Dave. But I do remember a woman sitting a few rows down the aisle from me in that airplane. Come to think of it, too, she was at the dinner I was at with Bermuda officers discussing Paulson's arrest shortly after I landed."

"Good—but Joe I gotta go. I'm being flagged by another agent regarding more drug dealing." Just before he could click off, however, Terry suddenly informed him: "Halleluyah Joe, what do ya know! I just found the name of that agent with Dave while flicking through my agent lists. It's Dana, Dana Goodwin. She's one of our younger agents who, incidentally, is also from the Mideast. I don't know much more about her. As you know, our agents operate mostly behind the scene. But the records I found show she's the one who was with Paulson in Bermuda."

Johnson clicked off before Kavinsky was able to inquire further about agent Goodwin. But he remembered now that someone called Dana was to remain with Bermuda police to help with the investigation of the Paulson death, and discuss possible international charges against other U.S. citizens involved with drug operations on that British island. This sure tarnished the image of an island long regarded as a place to escape from the troubles of life and to relax and enjoy its pink sandy beaches, Joe sighed.

Although Johnson seemed rather rushed in his conversation, enough was said to convince Joe that he should indeed call Dana in Bermuda soon, to find out the latest on how the Paulson investigation was going and the possible charges to be levied against his St. Paul accomplices in illicit drug operations. In thinking of phone calls, he also recalled he should try first to contact Salid's sister. His initial attempt at reaching her was frustrating, all he could hear was a busy signal. He left a voice mail message, but the response wasn't heard until several hours after Joe returned from his many other duties involving local police matters.

CHAPTER 4

Paola Murka left a number for Kavinsky to call, letting him know she got his message and would like to discuss it away from her "mother house." Joe took this to mean that she may be doing something without proper consent of her organization.

He immediately grabbed for the phone, but before he could put it to his ear his Caller-ID came up with the name *Dana*. Kavinsky paused, wondering who to talk to first. He decided that, rather than perhaps getting another voice message, it would be better to click onto the caller in Bermuda—who he presumed was on hand awaiting his reply.

In the meantime, Sister Murka was going about her morning rituals, beginning with prayers before the crucifix in her small, bleak room of the convent. Her fervent thoughts, however, were interrupted by wondering when detective Kavinsky would call back.

Moreover, she couldn't help being distracted thinking God was also being prayed to by so many others, perhaps at the same time, but in different ways, language and faiths, especially since the increase in terrorism, threats of revenge, and even war hovered around the world. Typical of many eager to reach God in the best way, she implored the Almighty to use her, to tell her what to do…tell her what to say.

She prayed intently, clutching a rosary while beseeching God that her sister be spared from an unjust sentence. Her worst fear was that Salid would be deported back to the terrible punishment inflicted on women daring to oppose the Taliban and al Qaida. She realized, from first-hand experiences, that they would like nothing better than to make an example of Salid for her betrayal by helping U.S. authorities upset some of their terrorist plans. She also knew that

Afghan law is based on Islamic principles, but stops short of extremist interpretation of Islamic law, known as Shariah, applied by the Taliban regime.

Upon rising from kneeling on the cold cement floor, Paola, garbed in a gray uniform depicting her religious order, but minus a habit over her head as most orthodox nuns wore years ago, opened an old photo album and sat back on her plain narrow bed. She flicked through pages of snap shots showing her and her sister in happier days, some when they romped through the woods and up some of the mountain slopes nearby their Afghanistan home. Their mother and her father, killed years ago by resisting the Taliban movement, were also pictured with their two little daughters and pet dog Shirlee who enjoyed chasing after the little girls.

She fondly remembered her mother requesting one of her sisters, a former Muslim who relocated in the U.S., to help protect her daughters should any harm befall them. Paola found a faded, tattered copy of her mother's letter asking for such help while moving from their humble dwelling to the foothills near Baghdad. Although her family escaped the onslaught of the Kurds by Saddam, the Taliban and a fifth column of mullahs and terrorists swarmed down upon their tiny town of Basra taking many parents away from their families for disobeying their harsh rules.

Both she and Salid were rescued by her Christian aunt who sneaked them out of their terrible environment. These horrible memories prompted Paola to become a legal alien after five years in the U.S. as a child and later find peace and security in a convent on becoming a Christian. Her sister Salid, however, declined citizenship and stayed nearly hidden with her aunt's husband who later left his wife over religious beliefs and reverted to his Islamic roots. Although his wife stayed a devout Christian, fostering this among her children, Salid, influenced by her adoptive father, remained a Muslim.

Salid, however, blamed both the father and her husband for introducing her to those in her faith wishing to undermine the U.S. power structure, believing that the American "Devil" was against everything Allah stood for. Some eventually turned to dealing in narcotics to help accomplish this, based on the theory that "Drugs Beget Terrorism" such as kingpins like Robert Beck, the notorious drug lord who was arrested while trying to terrorize the U.S heartland. However, Salid soon became aware of how they were using her, and cooperated with U.S. authorities, including the DEA and Kavinsky to capture Beck and his terrorists before they could carry out their deadly missions.

In return for her help, the authorities also promised Salid protective custody from the Beck gang.

But before departing, Paola cautioned Salid: "Be careful little sister, you have no rights as a woman where you come from, and very little here. Your right to live here expired with Amad's death and you are no longer considered a legal citizen of this country. In fact, you are believed by some to still belong to the Jihad, and the Taliban may soon try to get you for the severe punishment they believe you deserve."

Remembering these words and the fact that the U.S. was still trying to recover from 9/11 and probing any situation involving terrorism with great suspicion, Salid put her face in her hands and began weeping in her isolated cell. When she looked up, however, she was startled to find a face looking down at her.

The face was unknown. But it was smiling. The color of the skin matched hers, although the eyes were somewhat hidden by thick glasses. Indeed the overall persona of this visitor helped assure her that he was indeed one of her own kind and was there to comfort her.

"I am preparing to be your lawyer, Salid. There is nothing you should fear. The U.S. embassy is in the process of sanctioning me to represent you in court. I am familiar with your circumstances and will protect you from any unfair charges."

Salid's first reaction was to withdraw from this aggressive stranger, not knowing for certain if she should confide in him. When he sat down on the cot with her she instinctively moved away, wishing to keep her distance until knowing more about him.

"You must trust me, Salid. I am well acquainted with American law as well as that of our native country. I have all the necessary credentials to properly represent you during your upcoming hearing. I'm told by the INS that you are still a citizen of Afghanistan. But believe me, you will receive the justice you were pledged and deserve," he said drawing closer to the nearly trembling woman.

The words "deserve" alerted her to the warning of her sister. She recalled, that back in her desert home women were almost spat upon and "deserved nothing" but punishment if they did anything the Taliban frowned upon.

She recoiled again from his advances, and after wiping away her tears stared back at this soft-spoken man. It was as though he was too friendly—contrary to his supposed conservative upbringing and probably very strict attitude toward females.

"What is your name?" she asked rather protectively.

"Mr. Harim Nakeem."

He added, "Although I am from the Mideast I am considered so American now that some even call me Harry," he grinned.

Salid knew he was attempting to encourage her to be friendly, and politely returned his smile. "What do I do next?" she asked as thought testing his credentials.

"Sit here and contemplate your deeds. I in turn will quickly proceed to speed up your hearing and will keep you informed about my progress."

When her cell door clang shut, she could see Nakeem stop at the checkout desk, manned by another rather dark skinned person, and seemingly whisper something to him before signing the register. After he left, a strange and eerie silence prevailed that added to Salid's depression as the jailer kept staring at her—in an evil way, she felt.

While this was going on, Kavinsky was placing a call back to Bermuda to find out more about DEA agent Dana and the progress being made investigating Dave Paulson's still unexplained death.

This time, instead of hearing a voice-mail he heard a woman's deep voice announcing she was Dana. Moreover she immediately began chatting with Joe as though they were already close pals.

She explained, "No one seems to know much about Dave's death. The guard at the jail that night just took a 15-minute break, as scheduled, and left for a coffee break in the same building. When he returned, he found Dave with the knife in his back."

"When did you find out about it?"

"Shortly after you did. I was in my room at the Fairmont Southampton when I was finally notified. They told me at first it was a suicide. When I drove down to the damn jail, you had already met with those in charge and were boarding a plane to fly back home to confer with police and DEA officials," she said coarsely.

"Yes, I remember. I was told by the DEA you were to remain in Bermuda and check into this, as well as proceedings involving the charges against the two other accomplices, our former police chief and medical examiner, caught with him in obtaining illegal drug money." She responded, "Yes, they are taking up much of my time, since they became British citizens, but still had their U.S. citizen papers on them when arrested. The legal ramifications are twofold, plus I'm running into so many authorities from Interpol and officials from this colony that it's getting terribly confusing."

"I'm sure it is. His accomplices were also both after drug money dumped into the Atlantic by Zack Crimmons, and were quite aware that they could avoid any U.S. taxes by enjoying their loot as legal residents in sunny Bermuda."

Joe added, "And I'm sure Paulson also wanted to enjoy that lifestyle. But his life didn't last very long. There could be lots of folks who saw to that."

He didn't get a response. Dana said suddenly, and simply, that she had to click off to check something out and would keep in touch from Bermuda.

During their brief conversation, Joe took notes of what Dana was saying. Among his scribbling were the words: Fairmont Southampton. He vaguely recalled that this hotel was more commonly referred to as the Southampton Princess among taxi drivers, and that it was many miles from the downtown jail where Paulson was locked up.

In fact, he wondered why Dana would select such a place to stay so far away from the jail site if she was assigned to frequently check things out there for the DEA. He then made another note as a reminder to ask Terry Johnson about this.

His main focus, however, was still on the sad situation confronting Salid. He made this a priority over matters regarding Paulson's death. But his deep thoughts were interrupted by a phone call from his uncle Al, a popular local reporter still nosing around for news despite being 60 and limping slightly from a recent hip operation.

"Joe, how about you and your pretty wife taking time out to go to dinner with me and the missus tonight?"

This was a surprise to Kavinsky, knowing that Benjamin usually covered the evening news beat at the Minneapolis paper where he worked as one of their star reporters. "What's the matter, you been laid off?" kidded Joe.

"Nope, we've got a night out for ourselves thanks to some rookies who are learning how to gather news like us veterans," replied Al.

"Well, that'll take some doing unc. But I'm glad you can take a break. Sarah and I will be delighted to dine with you and auntie and get caught up on what's really going on around the town. And, who knows, I may be able to fill you in on some updates," Joe added jokingly, knowing that telling his aggressive journalistic uncle about anything he already didn't know about was nearly impossible.

Dining out with the Benjamins wasn't exactly the classiest occasion, especially in the mediocre steak house they recommended. But Joe and Sarah tolerated this in their usual humble manner even though they now were secretly regarded as millionaires. Sarah's dad, Zack Crimmons, was a wealthy lawyer who drowned by suicide in an area of the ocean near Bermuda where his terrorists associates were trying to recover some of his money. He left Sarah and her sister Susan with several million each, after taxes. Much of this was considered illegal drug money, but the remainder was described as legal inheritance.

The Kavinsky's kept their unexpected treasure confidential since it might bring further embarrassment to Sarah and disgrace to her father, the notorious swindler who became involved with drug smuggling and laundering in later life. The money they inherited, after much research by the IRS and legal and financial experts, was in a special trust fund established by Zack for his daughters.

Unaware of the Kavinsky's good fortune, Al protested somewhat when Sarah offered to pick up the dinner bill. On Joe's urging, she at least threw in enough for half the cost and Joe dug deep to leave a very sizeable tip.

"Your generosity is overwhelming nephew. This was suppose to be the Benjamin treat," shrugged Al. "We know you two must be drowning in expenses what with your new home and remodeling plans."

The word drowning made Sarah flush a little, thinking of her dad's drowning. Joe broke the silence since this may be right time to get Al's help and said, "My favorite uncle, do you know a good lawyer well versed in federal criminal and civil rights law. Someone you can really trust and rely on to be fair and just?"

"I've covered a lot of court cases, Joey, but there's one that may match up to that. That's Ralph Larson, a Scandinavian from Duluth. I've seen that guy in action and he can put the screws to you or take them off in a trial. He's very shrewd."

"Is he acquainted with our immigration laws?"

"Let me put it this way, Joe, if I needed to get in or out of this country legally and relatively easy, Ralph would probably be the one I'd use."

Al inquired, "Why do you ask? I sense that you're not telling your old uncle everything. Remember we work together very well, like a sleuth and a snoop. During my years of reporting I've come to know the good judges and lawyers from the not-so-good."

"Yeah, I realize that unc. How do I get in touch with this guy Larson?"

"You don't—he's always very busy. Let me do the initial contact work. But when do I get to know what you're after?"

"I'll inform you after I talk with him and find out how he can help."

"Can help with what?" quizzed Al.

"Help an unfortunate young lady behind bars being unfairly mistreated and probably soon to be deported back to a country where she may even be executed, that's all I can say."

"Whew!" was all his uncle could say. "It must be that pretty little thing you were trying to catch at the mall."

With that, Sarah looked sternly at her husband, remembering how she would tease him about flirting with this mystery woman to help round up terrorists in the mall.

"Yeah—it must be," she said nudging Joe. "Can't go into that just now," responded Kavinsky winking at his wife. "But I made some promises I want to keep—and I think all involved should try keeping."

In an effort to change the subject, noting his nephew squirming, his uncle asked about the status of the Paulson investigation. He also knew Dave quite well having worked with him in obtaining a story revealing the many VIPs in the Twin Cities collaborating with the drug world. Like Joe, he was shocked by the report that Paulson was the "mole" in the local police organization spying for the terrorists.

"We're still trying for a blood match on the knife. If we get that uncle Al…we've got our killer."

"Suppose Dave would roll over in his grave if that happens," Al commented.

Al's wife Kay suddenly interrupted with a slight cough and a reminder that this was suppose to be a cheerful gathering and not another cop-reporter type meeting. Unfortunately, however, she emphasized this at a time when dessert was served with a sauce that looked bloody red.

After a good night's sleep, assisted by the alcohol absorbed at the dinner, Joe arose from the bed he so lovingly shared with Sarah to quickly down some black coffee and a few bites of toast, kiss his wife, and dash off to his detective duties.

He was running a bit late and encountered quite a stack of papers already on his desk. Included were a couple of notes apparently jotted down by the precinct's secretary Liz who, as usual, beat him to work. One simply reported: "a Mr. Nakeem called—will call back later." The other was from his uncle, who, although many years older than Joe, was always more prompt. Perhaps that's why he's such a good reporter—the first to get the scoops, Joe figured. Al left a phone number to contact Ralph Larson.

Joe shrugged, wondering who to call back first. He knew what the Larson call would be about, but he didn't know anyone named Nakeem, nor the purpose of his call.

Buzzing Liz, sitting only a few doors down, was one way to learn more about the messages if there were any, as well as remind him about his appointments for the day. However, she couldn't provide any insight into what Nakeem might want, but figured his uncle just wanted to say hello. She also noted, "However there was one call that came in but quickly hung up when I answered. I remember the name on the caller-ID was a Dane or Dano."

"Dana—was that it?"

"You're right. That's who it must be."

"Was it long distant?"

"No—it sounded like a regular local call. I didn't hear any words but detected a very deep voice, like a smoker's, on the other end. He or she didn't leave a message. It just came up 'unavailable'—no number on the monitor to call back. Probably another telemarketer."

"She," Joe interrupted. "Dana's a she, Liz…with a gruff voice."

His secretary looked surprised. "Yeah", Joe reassured, "She's a DEA agent named Dana Goodwin." Liz kidded, "Does your wife know about these secret calls?" He didn't smile back since it was no laughing matter to Joe, who hoped the communications with Dana would soon help remove the secrecy lurking around who killed Paulson.

CHAPTER 5

❁

Joe pushed the note about Nakeem's call aside and resumed concentrating on his police projects for the day. As he started checking out some leads relating to more hold ups on the North Side in Minneapolis, he hardly realized his fingers were also flipping through the pages of the phone book.

It took a few moments to come across it—but there it was—a Harold Nakeem. He must have a little money, thought Joe, since his address was in a rather exclusive site overlooking one of Minneapolis' beautiful parks, a long way from the low-income residents in a northern resident he was checking out involving embezzlement.

Thinking a guy living in a high-class area was most likely a big shot, he recalled his dinner conversation with his uncle who said during his time as a reporter he became acquainted with influential people around the Twin Cities, including lawyers and the like, and if Joe ever needed a good 'mouthpiece' he could probably lead him to one.

This prompted Kavinsky to began flipping to the yellow pages. Sure enough there was a small advertisement on Nakeem Legal Services. Unlike most attorney ads, this was rather inconspicuous in a corner of a page—no photo or graphics, just a listing. However, under the name were the highlighted words "Immigration Counselor."

When he had a spare moment, Kavinsky dialed his uncle to obtain further names of lawyers who might best defend Salid. Upon reviewing a few of Al's references, including Larson, both nephew and uncle agreed that anyone who refers to himself as specializing in immigration law may be a darn good start in searching for the right guy.

Nakeem wasn't easy to reach, however. He left a voice mail telling the caller to try again the next day. Kavinsky thought it strange that a secretary hadn't answered to make an appointment, and also noted an accent in the voice...like someone from India or around there.

Putting his search on hold for correct legal aid, Joe once more became entangled in some of the Minneapolis crime scene as directed by the chief. It was while he was in the city courthouse checking out incidences that he nearly bumped into some of the lawyers rushing around hallways to their various courtrooms. As usual, a few were taking breaks as jurors were still deciding verdicts.

One of the more aggressive attorneys, a scholarly-looking young man with a notebook under his arm, recognized Kavinsky before Joe could spot him. He worked as an intern in Joe's police precinct while going to college prior to law school. Kavinsky always considered him an exceptionally bright young fella eager to learn the legal side of things from the cops on up.

"Leo, is that you? If so, I assume you're now an authentic legal eagle flying around a big jury case," Joe kidded.

"Yeah, I finally made it Mr. Kavinsky...with your help, of course."

Joe liked the praise, but was almost too busy trying to remember Leo's last name to respond quickly. Luckily, he spotted the notebook Leo was carrying about with his full name enscribed on the cover. It rang a bell for Joe. Morrison—yes, it's Leo Morrison—he was the studious lad working with him while pursuing a law degree.

"Congratulations—I figured you'd be doing some great things. What kind of cases have you been handling?"

"Quite a variety, but mostly criminal—in fact, right in your area of expertise Mr. Kavinsky."

"Please, call me Joe. I'm not surprised that's what you're into. We weren't able to scare you off the crime beat, eh Leo?"

"No way. I've been excited about it for some time."

"Are you mostly for the defense or the plaintiff," probed Joe realizing. Morrison probably had a very good success record in either case.

"I like being a defense attorney, Joe. But I might consider handling the prosecutor side, too. It would certainly add to my credentials. Defense is very satisfying, however,...you'd be surprised to know how many people are falsely accused and fill our jails with hardly any legal aid to protect them."

"Matter of fact, I believe I do, Leo. As you may recall, I'm usually right on the front lines, so to speak, in witnessing those who get in trouble with the law.

It's tough for me, too, to see some of the folks I believe to be innocent who end up behind bars."

With this, Joe's mind focused on Salid, an excellent example of perhaps being headed for prosecution unfairly.

"I have a person in mind right now, Leo, who I'm sure is being treated unjustly and could certainly use an excellent defense attorney. But I'm certain it takes a special lawyer…one who can understand a person with different beliefs and appreciate where they're coming from. Do you know anyone like that?" asked Joe.

"Some…but not many. You're right, at times it takes a lawyer who actually comes from the country of the defendant," acknowledged Leo.

"But, I do know attorneys who have background like this. In fact, I have some knowledge about it myself. Do you have anyone in mind?"

"Not exactly. About the only person I've found that may be up to this is one I noted from the yellow pages—a guy by the name of Nakeem."

"Not Harry Nakeem?" asked the young counselor almost stepping back in surprise.

"Yeah—that's the one. Do you know him?"

"Only by reputation."

"And what's that?"

"Questionable. And it's not Harry. It's some weird Mideast name. He has a strange track record, Joe, one that fellow lawyers wonder about."

"How come?"

"He's a counselor in his own world. I understand he was born in Afghanistan. Other lawyers have tried to get involved in his cases, but he seems to be the one selected by those who are immigrants, such as Muslims, you name it, believing he can find a balance of justice between the Mideast and West, aware of the clash between them."

"Why is this 'questionable'?"

"Most of the times, lawyers who had anything to do with him believe he may be deceiving his clients. I understand it's difficult to know what eventually happens to them, be it citizens or non-citizens."

Joe shook his head, wondering how people, no matter where they came from, would want a guy like that to defend them in a court of law.

"I suppose you're much too busy to take this case?" questioned the detective, trying to figure out how to protect Salid from such unpredictable attorneys.

"I haven't been appointed to do so. But there are some capable lawyers who specialize in such cases, and I may be able to refer you to some."

Joe jumped on this, recalling that his uncle mentioned the name of Ralph Larson, an attorney Al recommended.

"Is Ralph Larson one of them?" he asked.

Without any hesitation, Leo responded, "Maybe. He's got a good track record I understand. I don't know him very well but heard about him. For instance, he's supposed to be well versed in protocol and proper defense of people who may be under such injustice as ethnic or religious profiling. I've seen him in action. He usually wins his cases, no matter how biased they are," he noted.

"Thanks. Sounds like I should contact him, Leo. But could you be around if there's a problem that arises over this strange case—perhaps just to offer some advice to me?"

"Would be happy to, Joe. I sure owe you for all the experience and time you gave me regarding police matters."

Before rushing off to the courtroom awaiting his legal help, Joe's busy attorney friend left with a warning: "But I'll have to be well backgrounded about your case first." Kavinsky loudly responded back to the departing young lawyer, "You will be–I'll make sure of that."

Upon returning to his precinct, Joe once again began flipping through the large directory of numerous attorneys in the Twin Cities and suburbs. He knew, however, that Salid also was authorized to have a voice about who would defend her.

Finding Ralph Larson was relatively easy, even though there are many with that last name in the area. Unlike Nakeem's listing, however, Larson & Larson could be readily spotted thanks to the large display ad which pictured both Ralph and his brother Don. A caption under the pictures identified them as "experts in global law and international relations and procedures."

Joe at first was going to call his uncle to determine what exactly this meant, but looking at the work load building up on his desk relating to local police matters, he wrote the phone numbers of the Larson office down and was all set to attack his paperwork when the cell phone on his belt jingled.

"Mr. Kavinsky…this is Ralph Larson. I understand from your uncle Alvin Benjamin that you may wish to talk to me regarding someone who may be receiving unfair justice due to nationality and/or religious bias."

"Whoa!" was all Joe could say. He was amazed at how fast Al was moving on this matter without being prompted to do so.

"I would like to talk to you Ralph, but this has to be low-key. Did my uncle tell you about what's going on?"

"No, he simply phoned me and said he thought it would be a good idea to call you. He didn't tell me any details but said it was of a rather proprietary nature."

Kavinsky thought this guy sure talks like a lawyer. "Where can we meet to go over this?" he asked.

"My office is in the IDS tower and I could see you tomorrow afternoon if you wish."

Looking at both his watch and the stack of paperwork facing him, Joe at first was about to suggest later in the week, but remembering Salid's tough life in the marshal's jail he suggested visiting Larson's office first thing the next morning, before going to work. The lawyer didn't hesitate agreeing to this, noting the anxiety in Kavinsky's voice over the phone and that the detective may be investigating something he should know about.

Kavinsky's day went fast following this phone call. The chief had him also checking out some drug problems on the south side where lots of immigrants were struggling to get adjusted to American life without hardly knowing much English. Many were good targets for dope peddlers wishing to broaden their network of drug dealing around that area.

Joe couldn't help but feel almost as depressed as those he saw on the streets looking for answers to how they might find some sort of hope and happiness. He and his police companions were able to round up some of the more obvious dealers but they knew for every arrest, there were hundreds more out there handing out cocaine and other vile drugs, selling it or sniffing it.

He came home still feeling melancholy over his futile attempts at trying to reduce this increasing drug business which brings so many bad things to so many tempted to try it. He began to think about Adam and Eve who went down thinking an apple was good offered to them by a snake.

Sarah quickly detected his glum mood and suggested they go to a light-hearted movie that night, one both humorous and romantic, noting that she could get a reliable sitter for their baby Matilda. Once he sat down to enjoy the pleasantness of home, however, he was not inclined to break away. He also recalled his early meeting with lawyer Larson early the next morning.

Following a nice dinner, along with their favorite wine, the couple relaxed and talked about things far removed from the ugliness Joe often encounters in his work. Sarah told him about her day with the mischievous baby and about her at-home computer work for Nieman Marcus as a part-time fashion advisor. Although she didn't need the money, she enjoyed the work. With this uplifting mood, both went to bed, after the baby was tucked into her crib, and quickly fell asleep, each with a contented smile after passionately kissing one another goodnight.

CHAPTER 6

❀

Morning came with a drizzling rain. Driving through this, plus the ground fog and heavy traffic on the freeway to Larson's office put Kavinsky's mind into a dark funk again. He had to account for his time at the precinct, of course, and hoped that he wouldn't be tied up with a long-winded lawyer most of the morning.

Unlike what he expected, Ralph Larson was sort of an eye-opener. He personally greeted the detective with a vigorous handshake at the door, mentioning it was still too early for his secretary to be on hand. Somewhat folksy, he seemed like he could win over any jury, no matter how judgmental.

Putting Joe finally in a good mood, the cheerful middle-aged defense attorney poured him a cup of coffee and then sat behind his desk waiting to hear what the cop had on his mind. After explaining the situation regarding Salid, Joe sat back while Larson rose from his chair and lit a cigar. Exhaling some smoke, he appeared to be in deep thought before commenting on what he heard.

"It's a very sensitive predicament Mr. Kavinsky. For one thing, when you're dealing with a non-citizen accused of harboring terrorists and then joining them in their plans to commit crime I'd say we have more than our hands full to get them off with anything but a long prison sentence—no matter what kind of plea bargain we brought to the judge."

The detective interrupted, "Please—call me Joe. I realize this is very complicated, but both federal and local authorities promised this young lady leniency for helping to arrest the terrorists. And I don't think she's getting it."

"And your question is—why not?"

"Exactly. And I'm here because I've heard about your reputation in protecting the innocent, especially those being mistreated because of race, religion, or what have you."

"But this is something very different, Joe. Having spent a little time in Afghanistan before 9/11 and encountering some of those in Taliban country and the breeding ground of Osama, I would say these folks aren't about to sit back without trying to get this woman returned to them for punishment They're vindictive and would like to make her an example."

"Do we have a chance to protect her?"

"It'll be an uphill fight. I'm sure they'll use every trick imaginable to get her back home to show others that no woman should ever be so disloyal—and the terrible consequences to them when they do."

"What do we do?"

"Let me think more about this, Joe. I have a lot of advisors on such delicate matters requiring a very smooth hand. It may take me some time to determine how to proceed with this. But I'm willing to represent her. Where is she now?"

"Locked up in a very gloomy detention cell in a lower chamber of our federal building. That's why I'd like to move ahead as fast as possible."

With that, Larson sat back in his big chair, snuffed out his cigar, looked at Joe and surprisingly said with a rather mischievous smile. "There's nothing going on between you and that woman is there?"

"Ralph, again—I only want justice to be served, as we promised. Believe me, I'm a very happy married man with child and have no desire other than seeing her kept away from further mistreatment."

"And kept away from punishment," added the lawyer. "She would have no chance if she's deported."

After a long pause, Larson looked at the calendar on his desk and said "I believe I can get at this faster than I thought. But it's important that no other lawyer get to her and that she's willing to confer with me and follow my advice."

"I'll be sure to let her know Ralph. As far as I know, she hasn't any visitors."

"Good, and instruct the marshals to get the names of anyone inquiring about her or wishing to see her. This has to be controlled rigidly, Joe, making sure the wrong people can't get to her."

"I hear you. I'll tell the marshal to set up a strict checkin-checkout system. However, you realize I can't push them down there. They're a federal bunch and take orders from a different boss than a police chief."

Larson nodded in agreement and checked his watch, indicating that it was about time for Joe to leave. "I appreciate your help. Tell them I'll be setting up an appointment to see her. We don't want anyone to interfere," he said suddenly opening his office door as if saying goodbye.

Joe felt like he was being ushered out before he could cover all the points he wanted to make. One thing he needed to ask was when would this busy lawyer find the time to visit Salid. But he figured he could call Larson back later in the day after the lawyer had a chance to catch up on some of his work. Kavinsky couldn't help but notice that the pile of papers on Larson's desk almost topped his own overflowing mail box, which prompted him to rush back to his precinct office to make sure the chief thought he wasn't neglecting this mounting pile of paperwork.

As soon as Joe departed, Larson returned to his desk, closed his window blinds, removed a black book from a bottom drawer and used a key to open the latched book cover. He then flipped through many pages before finding the information he wanted—a phone number highlighted and marked "very confidential". He then bolted his office door and slowly dialed the number. He loosened his bow tie before whispering: "Abdul—there is still hope. Salid should soon be returning to the Taliban."

Kavinsky wasn't as fortunate to have the privacy Larson had. In fact, the chief, as well as all others strolling by Joe's cluttered desk at the police station, couldn't help but spot one of his new papers—a Post-it note on his phone which plainly let them know that he was involved that morning with something other than police matters as well as being late for work. It was dated while he was at Larson's office and read: "Call the marshal's office as soon as you return from the lawyer's."

Joe hesitated at first, looking about to see some of the smiling faces ready to kid him about his tardiness. Most appeared rather sheepish, and quickly looked back at their own assortment of paperwork rather than commenting. One, however, shared glances with him—Liz, the station secretary, who realized she shouldn't have placed the note so prominently in sight of passersby.

Before he finished dialing the marshal, the cell phone on his belt next to his gun jingled loudly further capturing the attention of those around him. He didn't know who to talk to first, but when he saw the monitor come up with "TJ"—the code name of his DEA friend Terry Johnson—he immediately clicked onto him.

"Joe, hope you're sitting down," was Johnson's opener. Kavinsky was almost afraid to ask why. The reason was given quickly. "We need that knife of yours again. Our DNA boys want to further examine it as soon as you can get it to them at our lab."

"What's up Terry, why the rush?" he asked. "Can't say for sure. But our agent Dana hasn't returned yet from Bermuda…no one knows for sure what happened. "Joe caught on to what Johnson was saying rapidly. "You mean she may be a suspect?"

"There's lots of questions to answer. Just bring that knife with you as fast as you can." Terry demanded. Joe thought, "Damn, here I go again on another rush from my office." Only this time he made certain to walk by Liz and whisper that he had another assignment and not to tell the whole precinct of his whereabouts—at least not with a poster-sized Post-it note.

CHAPTER 7

Joe put his hand in a glove and very carefully removed the knife, enclosed in a plastic bag, from a sealed cabinet labeled *important evidence*. He then nonchalantly walked by the other detectives who wondered where he was off to next, following him with their eyes as though he was a suspect. On his way out of the door, he intentionally looked back at his teasing pals and said "boo!"

The meeting with Johnson was unlike most of his contacts with this covert friend. This time, instead of conferring with him in an out-of-the-way restaurant or other type hideaway, Joe was allowed to enter the DEA building and dash up to his office. Everything was pre-arranged for his visit, with the guard at the desk waiving him on.

The moment he arrived, Joe plunked the knife on Terry's desk.

"Boy, that's quite a dagger," Johnson declared, after reminding Joe that it must be stored by federal authorities. "It sure wouldn't take too strong a person to put that in your back."

"Even a woman," agreed Kavinsky nodding his head.

"Yeah, even a woman. Maybe even our sister Dana."

"Have you found her yet?"

"Nope—but we're sure looking. Our contacts at Bermuda are trying to trace her down. For what its worth, hopefully there's enough DNA evidence still on this blade to find out for sure who did it to Dave. We know most of it must be his, but sometimes the stabber gets cut, too. If so, we can get a reading on this."

He continued, "It should take only a day or so, Joe. Our department already has bloodwork reports on all our agents, it's required to get the job. We had no idea, of course, that we'd have to re-take this, but then again we had no suspicions about Dana at the time."

"What makes you have any now?" asked Joe.

"Believe it or not, we have some reports that Dana and Dave were very good friends. Lovers, in fact. When we sent her over to Bermuda to check him out for possible federal charges we had no suspicions that there was anything between them. Damn, Joe, those two were seeing one another on the side for a long time. Since they were both law enforcers they were able to pull this off very discreetly, behind our backs."

"Speaking of backs, Dave really got it in his," Joe noted. "Could have happened when they were embracing in that cell of his," Johnson guessed with a shrug, adding, "But then, we're just speculating. It may have been someone else who got him. There was no one near his cell that late at night. It was a perfect setup for his murder."

CHAPTER 8

※

"No suicide?" asked Joe rather surprised.

"No way," replied Johnson emphatically.

Assured that Terry would let him know immediately when the DNA report came back from the lab, Kavinsky walked out of the DEA department and was driving back to his station when he remembered to call Ralph Larson.

Fortunately, he had already installed Larson's number in his cell phone and was able to quickly contact the lawyer's office. He tried concealing his use of the phone while driving by covering it with the hand he wasn't using to steer with. He knew this was risky and frowned on especially being a cop, but figured he had to do it considering all the projects he was facing that day as ordered by the police chief.

Hearing the phone at the other end being picked up he said simply, "Mr. Larson—what's up?" assuming Ralph would remember his voice. However, surprisingly a female voice responded. "Mr. Larson's in conference right now. I'm his secretary and will be pleased to have him return your call."

"Tell him Joe Kavinsky called him back," Joe said checking his watch, wondering if by now chief Hermes was already getting impatient looking for him.

The secretary seemed quite pleased to hear from him. "Oh, yes, Mr. Kavinsky, he's expecting you. I'll get him right away. Please hold for just a moment."

Impressed by this prompt action to get Ralph on the phone, Joe thought there must be something very important for Larson to tell him. This wasn't like the rather calm and cool attorney.

"Kavinsky—I thought you said you wouldn't let anyone know about our conversation to defend Salid." The angry and commanding voice of Larson, completely out of character for such a legal type guy, almost caused Joe to lose his grip on the phone.

"I didn't. Who said I did?"

"Never mind that!" Replied Larson totally losing his nice-guy image. "I found out that Nakeem visited with her in her cell," he bellowed. "Remember, if he becomes her lawyer—I'll resign the case."

"You haven't got the case yet, Mr. Larson."

That's to be decided by the court involved with immigrant injustice," corrected the upset lawyer. "And I'm certain there has been some injustice done by even allowing that man in her cell."

About all Joe could say to try to control the out-of-control Larson was: "I'll check into it Ralph. I want to defend Salid as much as you do, perhaps even more."

"Then why and how did that shady ambulance chaser get involved?"

Upon explaining that he was as puzzled over this as Larson was, Joe took a deep breath after this shouting match and paused to figure out his next move. Each situation facing him seemed to be a major project. He realized the chief wanted him back solving local crime and Terry Johnson indicated he soon would know who put the knife into Paulson—and needed him to be on hand to help check out DEA agent Dana. And if that wasn't enough, one of the top lawyers in town now wanted a prompt report from him regarding why a suspicious guy like Nakeem got into the cell of a woman supposed to be under heavy security.

It was like tossing a coin to see what to do first, Kavinsky shrugged. His thoughts were mostly on the plight of Salid, however. He couldn't get the sight of her weeping while locked up in that isolated jail from his mind. To get a better fix on what was happening, he felt it was urgent to directly talk to the marshal.

"Joe, believe me, I really don't know how anyone got through our check-in station. We know the rules, of course—it's important that all visitors have proper credentials to visit any of our prisoners. And that goes for lawyers, too," said the marshal.

"Do you have his name on your sign-in sheet?" inquired Kavinsky.

"No—the only one who came in over the past 24 hours was her father."

"Her father? She told me her father was killed many years ago," the surprised detective responded.

"We didn't get a good look at him. He showed us his license and social security card. The prisoner didn't seem alarmed by his visit," noted the marshal.

"Was there anyone there witnessing what was going on, or who could describe him?"

"Just the jailer. He's sort of part-time. We have many other matters to take care of, you know. The entire federal building's activities seem to be our responsibility."

Kavinsky sighed, "Yeah, I know that feeling of having too much to do."

"Would you have your jailer give me a call? I can be reached at the police station or on my cell phone," requested Joe who then gave the marshal his phone numbers.

"You bet," replied the marshal, pleased to make amends, "and believe me I'll get to the bottom of this and make sure this never happens again."

With that assurance, Joe said thanks and once again stared at his phone wondering what to do next.

But he didn't have to wait long. His cell phone jingled again and brought "TJ" up on his monitor.

"Terry, did you get a blood match on the knife?" Joe immediately asked.

"Yep. No problem. Seems the DEA has a traitor in our midst."

"You mean…?"

"I mean that our entrusted Dana must have stabbed Paulson. We further learned that she and Dave had some romantic difficulties. He jilted her and she became like a woman scorned. Our files on her revealed that the bloodwork she had done to join the DEA is a perfect match with the blood on the knife."

"Whew!"—was only way Joe could respond.

"I hinted that there may be a match when I last talked with you. And luckily there was just enough blood near the handle to identify Dana's. The rest was all Dave's, of course."

"Wow, how you guys can work with such complicated evidence."

"That's what we do in our job," Terry said proudly shrugging off this project as though it was a daily occurrence.

Kavinsky shrugged, too, thinking about the similarities between this situation and the one involving Salid. He couldn't help but ask, "How could someone sneak into Dave's cell to do this?"

"The jailer must have left for coffee just moments before Dana came. His keys were still hanging on the wall near his desk. Bermuda jails are a bit different than ours, Joe."

"Not much," noted Kavinsky, who then told Johnson about the mysterious way a lawyer crept into Salid's ugly cell. But as far as Joe knew, at least at this point, the result wasn't nearly as serious as Paulson's outcome.

Terry couldn't be of much help with this matter, however. About all he could offer was a warning for Joe to be very cautious since he knew the Taliban would love to make an example of Salid for her betrayal.

"They have many disguises, as you know, and can weasel their way like a rat into almost anything to get what they want."

"I'll have my guard up. Remember, I'm used to catching rats," remarked Joe recalling how he and Johnson teamed up to catch one of the biggest rats of all, Robert Beck, who was trying to establish a drug network around the Midwest based in the Twin Cities.

"Okay, but watch it—those Talibans can be even more slippery than Beck," cautioned Terry.

After clicking off from Terry, Joe checked his watch and, with his mind still set on the word slippery, wondered how he could slip back to his office without the chief and his fellow gang of criminal catchers noticing once again his long absence from local police duties.

Before he could figure this out, however, he was once again interrupted by the loud jingling of his cell phone. The damn thing even vibrated in his pocket as though urgently wanting him to respond.

It was from the marshal's office again.

"Joe—thought you might like to know your friend down here has another visitor," announced the excited jailer.

"Not another lawyer?"

"No. It's her sister. This is really a sight to behold."

Kavinsky sat down, wondering when all the suspense of this frustrating day would finally end."

"She's kneeling down and Salid is lying prostrate on the cold, hard floor."

The detective figured this was probably some sort of ritual but, wanting to make sure, he decided to rush once more to the federal detention center.

Although it took about 20 minutes to get there, the two girls were still in the same positions. The marshal was right, it was truly an impressive sight. There was Salid bowing on the concrete floor mumbling to God, while almost next to her was her sister Paola kneeling and looking up at the dirty ceiling loudly praying to the Almighty for divine help.

"Well, they may have different faiths—but God is God," explained Joe to the rather befuddled marshal.

"Somebody will have to come to their help soon," he said sighing.

"I think it'll be that lawyer Larson," guessed the marshal. "Larson called shortly after I contacted you and said he would be visiting the prisoner later this morning."

"Is he her official defense attorney now?"

"I asked him that, too. He told me he's been recommended by the International Court of Justice—an arm of the United Nations—to get involved."

"Wow," was all Joe could say, thinking Ralph apparently has lots more clout than he realized.

"When's he coming?"

"From all indications late this morning."

Kavinsky shook his head, once again looking at his watch. "I wish I could be there, but legally speaking I can't be between lawyer and client at this stage. Besides, as a fellow lawman, you know there are many other projects we've got to check out."

Nodding in agreement, the marshal said "I'll try to keep my eyes and ears open as to what's going on, Joe. Just talking to Larson makes me think he's a pretty nice fellow who's out to help her as much as he can…but who really knows."

Returning to his precinct, Kavinsky was nearly covered by the giant amount of paperwork waiting for him. He spent about half the day reducing the load, with the chief smiling at him behind a nearby office window while his colleagues made sure to keep their distance since he appeared so serious and busy in attacking his projects.

He did take time out however during his lunch break to learn more about Ralph Larson. For one thing, he read that Larson carved out one of the more unusual niche law practices in the United States. He became known as an expert in primarily representing foreigners, citing violations of treaties and laws, and even taking their cases to tribunals to make certain they received justice.

Such credentials gave Larson considerable success and helped to open many prison doors for him to represent those accused of offenses to the U.S., such as Salid may be charged with. No doubt about it, shrugged Joe, this fellow was very smooth—in some ways maybe even too smooth.

But, as he pointed out to the marshal, it was okay to let Larson come and go but to be make damn sure Nameed is kept away if at all possible. Joe had a gut feeling that Nameed's main intent was to bring Salid back to the Taliban—but he could be wrong.

Try as he might, Kavinsky couldn't help but squeeze in some time for the DEA during his busy day. Just before leaving the precinct for home, after making a small dent in his police work, he tried clicking onto Terry's cell phone.

His first attempt at reaching his covert pal brought only a busy signal. It wasn't until he got in his car and tried again before turning on the ignition that Johnson answered. Before he could even say who it was, Johnson, with the help of his caller-ID responded: "Joe, I know what you're thinking—we'll know more about Dana tomorrow."

"Why tomorrow?" questioned Kavinsky. "Because that's when she'll be back with us. The DEA has her scheduled for questioning in our interrogation room, and, believe me we intend to get all the details about her and Paulson."

"Am I invited?"

"If you wish. However, we have our own recipe for grilling our DEA birds who don't fly right."

"I've witnessed the worst, Terry. I believe I owe Dave the courtesy of watching her squirm. Why the hell could she be so mean as to stab him in the back while pretending to be his lover…"

"We run into lots of back stabbers, Joe, just like you regular police guys do. It's part of the job. But, I agree, she could have just left him with a powerful slap."

Kavinsky paused before continuing this conversation. He spotted chief Hermes coming to his desk with a frown as though ready to scold Joe for not paying enough attention to his job. But despite this, and feeling the importance of knowing more about the Paulson/Dana affair, Joe was able to conclude by saying: "Count me in—I'll be at your interrogation meeting Terry."

Chief Hermes quit frowning when told by Joe that the city's north side drug problems were being sharply reduced by the help of his police strategy. What's more, the chief smiled, when informed that Paulson's alleged killer was finally caught.

"But what about that Muslim girl you brought in?" Hermes asked.

"She's still waiting to be charged, chief. It's a question now of who will be the mouthpiece defending her."

CHAPTER 9

❦

Salid embraced her sister as they sadly bade farewell after arising from praying tearfully to God in the dismal cell for Salid's fair and quick release.

Although both had somewhat different upbringings, each understood the unique commonalities of humanity. As children of both West and Mideast cultures, they could accept the differences of both sides. However, as Salid told Joe when he visited with her later, "I think in Arabic, feel in Arabic, and can express and write in Arabic. But if I have a problem, I use my Western side. My logical side is Western."

"Do you communicate well with Nameed, do you see his side?" Kavinsky asked, realizing this was a lawyer also acquainted with both the Mideast and West.

"So far, he has treated me well. But I must say, there is something about the man that frightens me."

"I know what you mean," said Joe with a grin.

"How about Larson?"

"He also has treated me well. However, I am not yet convinced of his sincerity. Perhaps that will improve as I talk with him further."

"Hopefully," said Joe with a shrug, realizing that Ralph at this point seemingly was the best and final hope in her defense.

"Are you seeing him from your side or his?" he asked recalling her remarks about her two-sided cultures.

"From my western side."

"Your logical side?" inquired Kavinsky a little relieved over sensing that she's not siding with that shifty foreign fella Nakeem he was so nervous about.

Salid simply nodded. "Yes, but as you Americans like to say, the 'gut feeling.' also enters into this."

Realizing Larson would probably be furious again if Nakeem sneaked past him on this matter, Joe was still hesitant to mention Salid's feelings to him, although his his gut feeling was Ralph may still be the better of the two counselors—and, most of all, one who may be trusted a bit more. But he still couldn't help feeling unsure about this.

Kavinsky at this point figured he also needed a little counseling. And when it came to woman troubles, he knew just who to go to—his cute little wife who was busy changing diapers in their love nest.

Joe often marveled over Sarah's ability to interpret the female mind. She admitted, however, being a bit baffled by Salid at first. She vividly remembered when the pretty Muslim girl kept calling Joe on the phone at night letting him know where the terrorists were headed on their way to a secret meeting in the Twin Cities.

"What do you think she should do?" he asked his wife who was picking up bits of cereal playfully tossed on the floor by baby Matilda, who just recently was offered solid food after considerable nursing. Amazingly, Sarah, despite all her motherly duties, offered an immediate solution.

"I recommend you let her go with her instincts, no matter what you think. But I'm no mind reader Joe, especially when it comes to interpreting the thoughts of a woman so far removed from our way of life".

"She seems sold more on that guy Larson. But then again, she told me that she somehow questions his sincerity," Joe noted frowning.

"Why would she say that?" quizzed Sarah finally standing erect after picking up the last crumbs Matilda had thrown from the high chair as dog Stella carefully watched in hope of catching a few more.

Joe shrugged, "I don't know yet. But maybe I should check that out."

He added with a frown, "I must say Larson's whole attitude seemed different when I informed him about Nakeem's visit to her cell. He changed from being a mild-mannered guy to a pompous ass who didn't want anyone standing in his way."

"You should know the type…working with all those different characters in your line of work," Sarah mused, patting her husband on the shoulder to reinforce his feelings about this.

"Yeah—but I just can't get over how Larson changed from Mr. Nice to Mr. Hard-Nose. He never once thanked me for bringing this case to his attention.

He'll probably make a bundle on this—plus all the great publicity resulting from it."

"If he wins," interjected his wife now wiping the baby's face still partially covered with cereal around a very mischievous smile.

"Oh, he most likely will. This guy's got a terrific track record honey. I'm still on his side. It's just that there's something about him I can't pin down. I really must admit I can't feel very comfortable with either one.

"But then again, maybe I also should keep my eyes open for a substitute if necessary. Larson may not be exactly what he seems." Thinking of another way, he said "I do believe, however, Salid could select—or even defend herself in court if she wishes."

With that, Joe got up from the breakfast table, wiped his mouth mimicking the baby, and kissed his beloved wife and Matilda farewell as he headed out for another very busy day of being a cop, federal agent, and who knows what else he may be asked to do.

He couldn't help but murmur while going out the door, "You don't have to be a superman to do this job, but it sure as hell helps."

Ready for just about anything thrown at him, Joe wasn't too surprised to find a couple of Post-It notes already on his computer upon arriving at the precinct. They notified him about two callers—one from his DEA buddy again and the other from an "R.K. Larson."

He looked about to see Liz, but even she was late that morning. Someone else may have attached them. They were dated differently, with the one from Johnson coming in a bit earlier than the other. So in this case, he chose to answer Terry's first.

"Are you sitting down?" were the first words Kavinsky heard from Johnson. "We lost our suspect Dana—she somehow escaped while being escorted back to St. Paul."

"Who the hell was bringing her in?" Joe asked wondering what careless escort would allow this to happen.

"Dana tricked our man when she visited the lady's room before leaving the plane. When he checked out why she was so late in returning, there wasn't a trace of her anywhere around that area. She just plain and simply disappeared."

"Any idea where?"

"No, that's why I'm calling you. You knew Paulson better than the rest of us…who did he pal around with? do you remember any of Dana's friends?…questions like that Joe are what we need to explore. Dana worked with us only a short time. She apparently falsified her entrance exam."

He continued, "She was unaware that we suspected her. "The only way she could have escaped was with the help of someone else. This must have been well-planned."

"Can I meet with you for lunch to discuss this Terry?" Joe interrupted. "Geez, I have so much work to catch up with here I can't leave my desk this morning."

Agreeing to a meeting time, Joe's next obligation was to contact "R.K". As he clicked onto his phone number he thought about how such initials aptly described the formal and rather arrogant Larson. He couldn't understand why his uncle could have recommended this guy since Al was so much an opposite.

While waiting for his lunch with Terry, amid all the variety of work he was into for the chief, Joe's detective mind kept going back to how Dana could have possibly disappeared. After all, the only way out of a restroom of an airliner in flight, other than through its door and into the passenger aisle again, would be through a window. He chuckled out loud over this, knowing that she'd have to have wings like an angel to leave anyway but out the door. And indeed, she was no angel. Further, typical of most airline restroom traffic, she probably would have been noticed by others waiting in line to use the facility.

Thinking of the restroom created a yearning for Joe to go for his break in one. He snatched a newspaper on his way to his favorite stall and while glancing through it spotted a headline including the name of Larson. It seems RK was quite busy in his specialty of successfully freeing the unfortunate foreigner facing federal charges.

In fact, Larson was recently heralded for his recent dogged determination in convincing a jury of the wonderful attributes of a Mideast client. It was a long and interesting case involving a young man from Afghanistan accused of helping to establish a large number of meth labs in the Twin Cities. Not being a citizen, Larson contended the poor chap was being unfairly treated by not knowing U.S. laws forbidding the establishment of clandestine drug operations. His arguments often closed by stating that the war on terrorism must not be a war on Islam. Many jurors selected in his trials, in fact, were from the Mideast.

Joe also read an article on the same page that drugs were becoming a very big business in Minnesota, with more than 200 drug-making labs busted recently. Such labs can be a bomb, flammable and capable of blowing at any time. Reminding him of the troubled Mideast, he referred back to the Larson story and noted that Ralph usually disputed the notion that his clients are unstable and that warlords and drug kingpins are beyond control. "Amazing" mumbled Joe. "How could this attorney be so darn clever, knowing the minds of terrorists and the like?"

While Joe was reading about Larson's impressive legal finesse, Terry Johnson was also saying "amazing" as he pondered over the mysterious escape of Dana Goodrich. How and why did it happen? He went over everything, from the time the suspect was escorted to the airport to when she excused herself to go to the restroom. When he checked further, he learned that she only had a cosmetic kit when entering the restroom that looked just like a typical kit with compact, lipstick, rouge, and other usual ingredients. She had explained rather jokingly that she wanted to look her very best when landing.

When Terry conferred with Joe about this he didn't seem too surprised. "She or he also got by me on the plane to Bermuda, remember?" recalled Joe. "You were the one who finally told me the true gender of this person—didn't you know when you hired her, or him—or 'it'?"

CHAPTER 10

"Don't treat this lightly Kavinsky," cautioned Johnson. "This agent always mingled with our guys and was considered to be one of them. Why or how her true identity was disclosed is still confusing to me."

He added, "But we have traced her steps as much as possible. We figure at this stage that when she entered the restroom, she unlocked the latch and allowed another person, probably a woman, to enter with some male clothing to disguise our agent as a man."

Joe accepted this only after much frowning and head scratching. "I suppose that could be. Anyone looking on this would just figure another woman was visiting with her. If it was a man entering, it could be a problem."

"Exactly. But it does point to the possibility that there were other accomplices with her."

"But wouldn't your escort spot her when she left the restroom?"

"Not if she was disguised so much that she couldn't be recognized. And it could be she went out another exit—maybe a back window. Remember the plane wasn't in flight yet. The more I think about it, Dana may be some sort of a transvestite."

"That's kinda scary, isn't it Terry? If she was that clever...you're probably lucky the plane she was about to board wasn't terrorized by her buddies."

Joe added, "and I'm rather lucky I can get on with my police duties without having to go to another interrogation session regarding your tricky agent."

"At least for now," said Johnson. "But don't worry, we'll hunt her down soon. And the escort is in for some scolding. I'll be sure to keep you informed and bring you in on this again."

"Thanks pal. But I'm not so busy that I can't take time to help catch the person who did my partner in."

Despite Johnson's disappointing news, Kavinsky's attention immediately focused back on Salid. Since he wasn't sure how she was holding up in her gloomy little jail cell, he called the marshal to get an updated report.

"Nakeem was here again, Joe!" were the alarming words from the marshal's mouth. "Believe me, he had all the right papers to meet with her…we checked and double-checked to make sure he was properly authorized to enter her cell. He added, "he's just as qualified to do that as that guy Larson. We couldn't stop him."

"We're you able to overhear anything?"

The marshal's voice bristled. "Damn, Kavinsky, you know that's against our rules. We have strict orders not to even get within hearing distance around the area where a lawyer and the accused are deliberating."

"Okay, okay…just thought you may have something to offer so our little prisoner has some chance to be charged fairly," the detective shrugged, realizing this was one of those days when nothing seemed to go right.

"Do you know when he's coming back to see her?"

"He didn't mention anything about that. You're right, he's a very strange guy. We'll be sure to question him more when and if he returns."

Joe was sure that Nakeem indeed would be returning. But he knew it was time to return to his stack of work again. His thoughts were interrupted, however, by some loud sounds at the TV set near the chief's office.

Since the outbreak of the war with Iraq and terrorism relating to 9/11 the old set was getting lots of attention from those around the water cooler at the station. Wondering why the viewers seemed so upset this time, Joe pulled up a chair and noticed the terrible treatment some U.S. prisoners of war reportedly were receiving from the enemy. This also reminded him of the tough treatment his Mideast friend Salid may be undergoing since being jailed on charges still pending.

In his mind, it was a crime just to be holding her this long without proper justification. The more he thought about this, the more he was tempted to call the U.S. Attorney General's Office. Go right to the top, thought Joe, rather than mess around with some local marshal apparently afraid to do anything not listed in the rule book. How long would it take before justice is served? and what will result after all the legal, or illegal, counseling by lawyers virtually unknown by Kavinsky? These questions were troubling Joe who realized the more time involved on figuring out answers, the longer the hardship Salid would be encountering as she eagerly waited for her plea to be honored.

He tried hurrying up some of his local cop work in order to pay more attention to Salid's plight. By mid afternoon he was at a point to call Ralph Larson again to get an update on the progress being made in preparing for her defense. Only this time he was put on hold by the lawyer's voice-mail. Obviously his secretary was out as well as Larson. But fortunately the voice-mail let him know that the lawyer could be reached at the marshal's office. Although Joe really didn't care too much for the arrogant "RJ" he had to give him an A-plus for being so persistent in keeping in touch with clients, especially in the case of the poor immigrant Muslim girl.

After a somewhat frustrating day, Joe was packing up to go home to his wife and baby daughter when the ringing of his office phone interrupted. He hesitated before picking up the receiver when noticing the call was from the marshal's office again. He wasn't looking forward to a long, and perhaps irritating discussion.

This time it was from a more compassionate, friendly voice indicating a desire to talk for awhile. It was the deputy marshal, George Frey. He had a comforting way of speaking although this time he seemed slightly nervous over what he had recently observed.

"Mr. Kavinsky—you told us to keep an eye on that lady prisoner we have down here and to let you know anything unusual."

"Yes, and did you?"

"Well, I thought it kinda strange that when that lawyer left her cell she seemed awfully upset. I would say even frightened. She wasn't at all in the same mood before he came here," George noted.

"How to do you mean?"

"She was almost in tears again. I could sense that she was downright scared of that guy."

"What did he say, or do, to cause this?"

"I'm not sure. But whatever it was turned her almost pale. She's still crying a little on the cot in her cell."

"Is she all alone now?"

"Yep. And I can't be of much help since I have so many other duties to do around here."

Joe could relate to that. "Yeah, I'm sure you do," he responded looking at his watch knowing that he may once again be late to enjoy a leisurely dinner with Sarah and Matilda.

"I'll be right down George…and tell her that. She surely needs someone around who will at least attempt to cheer her up."

"I'm with you Joe. That damn lawyer isn't at all what she needs. If he's the type defending her, I'd hate to think of the kind that wouldn't be. That fella isn't doing his job. Instead of protecting her like he should be, for some reason he just seems to be upsetting her as much as possible."

"It's that guy Nakeem—I told your boss about him. He has to stay away from her! He's up to no good." Joe nearly hollered.

There suddenly was silence at the other end.

"I don't think that was his name—the marshal though took the check-in slips with him. What does he look like?" asked the somewhat startled deputy.

"Dark skinned, rather heavy with a beard."

"Nope, this guy was white, slim, no beard and sporting a bow tie, a red bow tie."

The detective was getting confused. That matched up with Larson not Nakeem. "RK" was sort of a nerd, he wore a bow tie when Joe saw him and he was more stout than slim. The skin description was what confused him most, however. "Are you sure he didn't look somewhat like an Arab?" asked Joe to help him identify this mystery visitor.

"I'm sure he was a true Caucasian."

Joe was getting very skeptical about any truth existing in this whole lawyer matter as he sped to the old federal building to find out for himself what the hell was going on. When he arrived there was hardly anyone in the long hallway leading to the stairs to the marshal's office. In fact, about all he could hear were his own rapid steps on the way to the detention area, they seemed to create an eerie echo.

George the jailer was still at his post, waiting for Kavinsky and holding keys to Salid's cell. Joe had a hard time trying to see her, however, since she was sort of hidden away in a corner of the cell with beads in her hand.

The entire scene was rather gloomy. The jailer should have turned a light on in the cell at least, thought Joe. But perhaps she didn't want anything other than this very somber setting. It certainly fit in with her depressed appearance when he approached her to hopefully lighten up her mood, if possible. However, she remained silent even when he asked what was wrong. In fact, she wouldn't look up from her prayer beads.

"Did you have a talk with your lawyer?" asked Joe for openers. Salid looked away from him as though she didn't want to discuss the subject. "I cannot and will not talk about that man," she declared as if making a pledge to herself.

Joe thought out loud, "Who knows, you may be able to fire him."

CHAPTER 11

Although disappointed by not gaining any helpful information, Joe was pleased that he could make it home on time to witness Sarah attempting to feed the baby without messing up the kitchen. They both seemed resigned, however, to losing this struggle, with Matilda sitting in her high chair playfully getting a kick out of it all.

In between attending to the baby, Joe was able to update Sarah on his attempts to protect Salid from being mistreated. His wife was inclined to being a somewhat more compassionate listener, but was still a little upset recalling the Muslim girl's frequent phone calls to Joe when she was tipping him off about the terrorists meeting being planned in the Twin Cities. Besides being a suspected accomplice in this matter, Sarah sometimes felt this pretty young woman, although mostly covered in a cloak, had the "hots" for her handsome husband.

She was relieved when the phone rang, interrupting the food pick-up game Matilda seemed to be playing, and found out it wasn't Salid on the other end. Instead, the caller was uncle Al.

Knowing it must be for Joe, she almost automatically passed the phone over to him across the table. There hardly wasn't a time when something didn't disrupt their evening meal, she sighed.

"Joe—I just got through proofing our upcoming morning newspaper," Al announced excitedly. "You should see the big story on the expected charges against your woman terrorist suspect. Boy, they're sure putting it to her. I thought you told me she would be given leniency by helping you guys round up the Beck gang?"

Joe sat back so suddenly that his dinner-table chair almost tipped over. "What do you mean?—there may not be charges and they wouldn't be filed until complete consideration of her role in this matter and the plea bargain were concluded."

"Well, they must be concluded," summed up Al. "It says here that the court has decided to arraign her on being accused as an accomplice in helping to spread drug operations throughout the Midwest and for her role in promoting terrorism. That's what the preliminary hearing is all about."

He added, "Very mean accusations, I'd say, especially during an ugly war now being waged against all this."

"That damn Nakeem," was all Joe could utter. He thought this might be happening...but not so soon, realizing it was only a short time after Salid was visited by this strange attorney.

Questions were flowing in Joe's mind. How could her case be started without being more thoroughly investigated by local and federal authorities? And why was there such a rush to judgement?

At this point, Kavinsky was becoming thoroughly frustrated, not knowing what or who to check with for any answers. His mind flashed back to the steps already taken to help Salid, but apparently they weren't enough. However, in so doing, he recalled the meeting he had with his young ambitious attorney friend Leo Morrison.

Leo was easy to find in the phone book. Unlike Larson he didn't have his picture included along with the writeup. Joe thought Larson was a bit too egotistical. He couldn't pin it down, but felt uneasy about the guy although realizing he had more of a legal track record then Leo.

To ease his mind, Kavinsky decided to contact Leo. Looking about first to see if anyone was in ear-shot to hear his conversation, Joe called Leo's office although knowing the young man may already be making his rounds in the court house.

Surprisingly, he reached Morrison almost immediately, making him wonder if Leo wasn't perched at the phone waiting, and perhaps hoping, for someone to call with some business.

As usual, Leo seemed pleased to hear from Joe, who recalled Morrison was always pleasant even as a kid. A 'down-to-earth' type who took time to talk with you no matter what your rank in society might be. There was no artificial facade about this guy. He was just plain Leo.

"Got a problem Leo. Could you spare a moment at Maxi's restaurant this noon? It's about that young girl locked up in the federal building who I believe is being punished unjustly."

There was a brief pause, as though Leo was checking his calendar or watch, but the reply was quite definite. "Sure—I can make it. Always fun to be near the campus again—and Maxi's is always jumping."

He added, "What's up? You sound quite serious."

"I believe she's being falsely charged and headed toward a hearing and trial that's already been decided against her."

"Gosh!—that sounds interesting. I do remember a little about this from our recent discussion. Have you tried Larson yet for some help?"

"Yes, but I have some questions and believe you're the best to talk with."

"You've always been a good investigator and an up-front guy Mr. Kavinsky. I'll be looking forward to our meeting. Please bring along anything you have on this case that could help me check it out."

Unknown to Joe, the case against Salid was already being readied by the federal judicial system even before he finished talking to Leo. In fact, one of the best known former federal prosecutors was approached to handle this controversial issue.

At least, thought Joe as he hung up and scheduled himself to lunch with Leo, Salid should not be a candidate for military tribunals set up to try terrorists nor could she be charged with treason since she's not a U.S. citizen. And, as Leo noted, she really isn't an illegal alien legally and probably can't be deported as Larson would want.

He struggled with reasons for not honoring her plea. Hell, thought Joe, instead of being threatened and admonished she should be given a medal for bravely helping to catch the notorious druglord—known by many as "Beck the Bad".

After all, he reasoned, Taliban law isn't calling the shots. It can't rule on punishing her severely without fairness...as it does with most women. Instead, if demanded, she would hopefully be facing an understanding hearing, and if necessary a jury—composed of open-minded, loyal citizens outraged by the Taliban and most likely very grateful for her cooperation in helping to chase down terrorists.

With his mind filled with all this fair-play logic, Kavinsky encountered the usual crowds at Maxi's and began eagerly searching for the usual-smiling face of his friend Leo. Being well organized, the young ambitious lawyer had already reserved a booth and, like Joe, was looking around to welcome the aggressive detective.

When both were finally sitting and facing each other, Kavinsky opened the conversation by directly asking: "Can you be at her hearings?"

"Her—being your Muslim friend I assume," responded Leo. "I'd like to, but as I mentioned on the phone I would first want to read up on this case. If you suspect something wrong please let me know now what it is and I'll be especially aware of this and be on guard so to speak."

"Good—and I hope I can speak to you about it in strict privacy. I've always regarded you as trustworthy and respecting confidential information, as I'm sure most of your fellow lawyers who know you would."

Leo blushed somewhat, and said "You can count on me. I'm rather ashamed too that there are some who are not very honorable and downright deceitful."

"Like maybe Harim Nakeem?" asked Kavinsky recognizing this as a good time to mention his name.

"Perhaps. But then again I've heard some good things about Nakeem lately. I'n fact, I've sort of changed my mind about him. He's also considered a good closure of cases and influencing jurors."

"And Ralph Larson?…is he still high on your recommendation list?"

"To a point. I really haven't seen nor heard him in action, but as I indicated to you earlier, some like his style, but others wonder about his ethics at times. He can be very stern and even blunt if he doesn't get his way I'm told. Maybe he has to be with his type of clients—mostly foreigners. I know nothing about his strategy—but if he's going to protect this woman he'd better use some tact and treat her as she deserves. The more you describe her, I would most definitely like to sit in on the case."

He emphasized, "I also suggest that she become more proactive. After all, Salid can choose her own lawyer or defend her case if she's not pleased. And you're right, she can even fire the ones now wanting to handle it. The prosecuting lawyer, of course, would be authorized by the Attorney General. What's the press been saying, by the way?"

"Perhaps my uncle's newspaper can tell you more," said Joe showing him the morning's Tribune. One of the main headlines focused on the pending charges and possible trial, in big bold print.

"Wow—I guess I didn't notice. I subscribe to that other paper and there wasn't even a mention of this."

"Well I'm sure my nosy uncle got another scoop to his credit. He covers the courthouse beat very carefully as a reporter."

Glancing at his watch, Leo said "Speaking of the court house I just remembered I must be at a hearing in a few minutes. But I'll be sure to read this. And incidentally, the INS could send her home immediately if there's a visa problem but not if her life's in danger. She's protected by the Human Rights Law if fear of retaliation."

Rushing off after quickly downing some soup and a sandwich, Morrison reminded Kavinsky to please let him know the time and day of the woman's hearing. "I sure want to get a good front-row seat for this one," he remarked waiving farewell.

Leo left Joe wondering how this hurried attorney could squeeze anymore into his very tight schedule. But he figured when you're trying to compete in the world of criminal law you've got to move fast. The old saying "ambulance chasers" certainly might describe some of those trying to get to the judge first, Joe realized But who's going to be the judge involved with this case? And when will it be on the court docket? These were added to the many questions Joe couldn't find answers to in uncle Al's article. So his next step was to call Al to get more information for Leo. As Joe went out the door of Maxi's he realized that perhaps he also was running around too fast and maybe should slow down for his own good.

However, contacting Al paid off. His uncle did have more input that didn't get into the early issue of the newspaper. Seems Benjamin returned late from his news beat just before the presses began running and didn't have time to complete some stories.

"I scribbled down some additional notes. Looks like there may not be a grand jury on this one, Joey. Once charges are listed it's apparently possible to go directly to a trial and from there possible sentencing," Al explained.

"That does seem strange unc. But then again this whole situation is strange. I just hope we don't have a strange judge involved."

"You might say we do, Joe. I'm told that the one selected for this is no other than the ultra conservative, and very patriotic but unpredictable Charles Mandy."

He noted, "As you may recall, however, Mandy's been known to drift from the rigid interpretation of the law at times. For that matter, he may have had a role in lifting the requirement for a grand jury in this case. A hearing's necessary—it's a state law. He can even send the case to a court of appeals as a federal district judge of Minnesota."

"Yeah, I also expect public opinion may be on his side in this one with the war and terrorism." cautioned Joe. "Seems many want to take their vengeance out on anyone even slightly suspected of aiding or abetting those who may be threatening the nation."

"And your gal Sal sort of falls in this category, you gotta admit," noted Al.

"The only thing wrong about that, though, is Salid tried to help us. Without her assistance, terrorism connected with drug operations could now be twice as bad around the Midwest and perhaps our entire nation," noted Kavinsky.

"I just hope Mandy makes a note of that. He shouldn't come down too hard on her, especially knowing the plea bargain. There's too many wanting to make an example of her...especially the Taliban who I'm sure will be very interested in the outcome of this case and are waiting to get their hands on her."

No doubt about it, the risks this woman faced were certainly all around her, thought Joe as he headed once again back to the precinct. He was still disturbed about all this during most of his work day despite the distractions he encountered with the increasing crime on the north side relating to drugs, race and even religious beliefs.

He realized that religion also can be entangled with the war on terrorism. And terrorist attacks claimed to act in the name of everything holy. Clearly this abused religion. There was something very wrong in all this, he concluded as he lit another cigarette and sat back in his chair realizing he could never solve this problem as a frustrated detective in a tiny cubicle. But he was somewhat comforted knowing that most Americans are trying to understand all aspects of the war, including the religious elements and that their values of defense are assuring freedom of religion.

Joe was certainly no philosopher, but he knew from experience that punishment can be overdone if based on some exaggerated accusations without proper and careful investigation.

His thoughts turned to the strict law of the Taliban. Those who violated it were punished severely. He shuddered to think what they would do to Salid if she's ever returned to her homeland.

Although they apparently wish to mirror the Biblical era, the Talibans really reflect a great contradiction to holy scripture in many ways, he felt. Joe could recall his mother scolding her kids when they were scrapping with one another and reminding them of a Biblical passage that went something like this: *"Vengeance Is Mine Sayeth The Lord"*. And these guys certainly weren't exemplifying this, he shrugged.

Many Taliban fighters in fact were now holed up in mountains in southern Afghanistan where they fled because of the war. But they were reportedly already reorganized once again with probably more vengeance than ever. Joe was sure they would like to get back to flogging their rebellious veiled women.

However, he still couldn't help but feel a little desire for vengeance himself whenever he thought about Dave Paulson's killer being on the loose. No one seemed to know where she might be hiding. He was still brooding about this when Terry Johnson called him from the DEA office.

"Joe did your uncle tell you about that picture in the Trib today?"

"There's an awful lot of photos in that paper Terry. Sometimes I think Al should help his wife more with her knitting. He's got his nose in that rag of a newspaper too much. I've given him a break in keeping me up on all the latest news but I don't know what picture you mean."

"Well, maybe you should take a look on page 3. There's a photo there of a crowd celebrating spring break in Florida. The kids are out in front whooping it up, with the folks in the background laughing at their antics."

"And so?" asked Joe knowing Johnson certainly didn't call him to tell him about the wild spring breakers. "And so, one of those bystanders is very familiar."

"Who would that be?"

"I'm not positive Joe, but I think it might be our agent Dana standing very far away from our other agent Gloria Marks."

"Wow!—you're amazing!. Can we trace this down to find her?"

"We're sure as hell going to try. I'm having some research done right now also regarding the people around her."

A taste for vengeance seemed to be swallowing up the world, thought Joe. Dana Goodwin was another good—but really bad—example. She expressed it by stabbing Paulson in the back. Which again reminded Kavinsky of being extra careful these days of watching your back when dealing with terrorists.

Regardless of Terry's plans to check out those in the newspaper photo, Joe had figured that his uncle, being a longtime investigative journalist, could also be helpful in finding out more about this through his contacts in the wire-photo news service and other sources his newspaper relied on for national news. He stressed the importance of keeping this matter confidential to Al who began immediately to snoop into where exactly the photo was taken and who may have given it to the wire service.

With both Johnson and Al looking into this, Kavinsky felt somewhat relaxed as he cuddled up to his wife that night and heard some little contented sighs via the intercom from the baby in the crib next to their room. It sure could be a wonderful and peaceful world, Joe thought before dozing off, if only so many people didn't hate one another.

As usual his uncle didn't get to sleep until very late. Being on a morning paper often meant calls and visits to the police and sheriff offices to catch up on crime happenings for the first edition. Most of this was routine that night, however, and fortunately Al found a little time to check into the mysterious photo Joe called about.

With the help of a thick magnifying glass, Benjamin closely examined the picture. The suspect was difficult to find behind the crowd of merry makers at the Florida resort area. There were four women in the background and Al had to figure out for himself who was the one the cops were after.

There was only one that Dave Paulson might be turned on about, decided Al. After all, he figured he knew some of Dave's quirks about the opposite sex. It would be the gal in the middle…the one standing behind all the others with her hand almost hiding her face. There was enough of her face shown, however, to know that she was the prettiest of the bunch. All wore bikinis and were apparently cheering on the spring breakers also scantily clad and teasing their boy friends.

He could see why a newspaper photographer would want to capture such frolicking. It's certainly good publicity for the resort, although probably worrying some parents back home. He used an even more powerful magnifying glass attempting to find out the sender of the photo. He did…it was from the Associated Press desk in Miami.

A phone call to a fellow reporter at the AP in Miami led him to the photo editor who knew immediately the name of the photographer. The editor, in fact, assigned the photographer to the beach with the reporter to cover the partying of these breakers.

Tyrone Pedersen was the photographer and Johnny Arneson the news writer, Al was told. He knew them both. They trained as rookies under Al's wing at the Trib. Arneson was out on his beat when Al was transferred to his extension, but Pedersen was still in the photo lab and came to the phone. He was glad to hear from Benjamin and after reminiscing about old times at the Trib, Al got right down to the reason for his call.

Where and when was this photo taken? and who were those pictured? were among questions Al zeroed in on right away. Pedersen said he'd have to study the photo again and put him on hold for a few minutes. In the meantime, Al kept looking at the newspaper picture and kept thinking he may have met the woman next to Goodwin some time ago.

"It was March ninth, Al…about mid day when the sun was out the brightest. It was extremely hot which made for too much glare," recalled Pedersen. I've got it all on record but don't have the identifications except for the kids out front. I don't believe the others wanted to give out their names. Why do you ask?"

"Oh, just wanted to know if any were from up here?"

"None that I know. Gosh I sure would like to see you guys again, but my job with the AP has been going fine."

"I'm sure it is, you've always been a terrific photographer Ty. Maybe I'll be getting in touch with you again soon, who knows?" Al immediately notified his nephew about the call and the information he received from the photographer. Joe took notes and then called Terry Johnson to update him on the picture in question. Johnson, in his role as a professional interrogator, had further questions including: "Where could the women onlookers be located? And are they still around the resort area.?"

"I'll have Al get back to you Terry—as you might know I'm jammed with local crime investigation at this time." Johnson replied, "Fine—I understand. It's tough being both a city cop and federal cover." He added, "But Joe—you don't have to try to get the lady's name pictured near Gloria and barely noticeable. We think we know her—she's also one of ours and, we suspect, one involved in Dave's love triangle."

CHAPTER 12

Johnson clicked off before Joe could find words to respond. About all he could do was scratch his head in trying to figure out what Terry was saying and what kind of organization the DEA was running if they had such weird and mysterious lovers among their agents.

As Kavinsky remained puzzled over this while still holding his phone, he sighed, thinking at least there certainly was no love going on between Ralph Larson and Harim Nakeem. For sure, they were most likely busy at this time fighting with one another over who would defend the young Muslim girl crying for protection.

Joe still was for Larson, although he didn't particularly like either. He would have preferred Leo, of course. But he was only a few years out of law school and may not be considered qualified for participating in such a high-profile trial dealing with special interpretations of immigration law and deportation regulations. There would be lots of press covering such a trial, he was sure, including his uncle Al.

Thinking of Al caused Joe to call him back to learn if he was able to get any more information on Dana from his pals at the Miami AP office.

"A little…Ty said they signed press release forms for him and included where they're staying. It's at the Monterrey near Collins Avenue—you know on the great Gold Coast."

"Could be a sham—a cover-up to where they're really at," said Joe. He asked Al, however, to pass this information on to Terry who would be waiting for his call and to keep him updated if possible.

"Are you that busy with that girl being held by the marshals? You usually want to be the one in contact with Johnson. Are you making any headway in her case?" asked Al.

"I'm even too busy to talk about that, unc. The chief is breathing down my neck to complete a report. But as for your question about Salid—no, I'm running into lots of unforeseen obstacles."

"But Joey the trial starts this week, remember?"

"How can I forget with you around?" said the impatient detective looking at the chief heading for his desk with another stack of work.

At least one worry off Joe's mind was knowing that his reliable uncle would follow through in keeping the DEA informed about Dana Goodwin. He sensed from Terry that maybe Dana was following the other agent to also do some harm to her for getting in the way of the strange romance that was going on between her and Paulson.

The weeks flew for Joe as he finally was able to make some progress in his police job, including rounding up some gangs of young dudes selling drugs and shooting at one another. He nearly forgot the upcoming Salid arraignment while keeping the chief happy with his local detective work.

Although he came home late again the night before Salid's hearing was to start, he told Sarah to set the alarm extra early to be sure he could attend the opening first thing in the morning. He wasn't asked to participate in any way, but he wanted to closely observe what would be going on. Despite his plans for sleep, however, he didn't nod off until much passionate love making with his beautiful wife in their comfy new bed. In fact, he was still a bit sleepy even after downing lots of black coffee when he arrived at the large paneled courtroom on the third floor of the federal building.

Immediately upon opening the big wooden doors leading to the judge's bench he spotted both Nakeem and Larson. However, Larson was sitting where the defense attorney sits and Nakeem was out in the rows with other attendees. What was going on? Joe was also wondering who did the attorney general finally authorize to be the prosecuting lawyer representing the government?

Everyone became silent and stood up when the judge appeared. They all followed proper protocol and sat in sync with Mandy. It was easy for Joe to spot his uncle near the front row and notice that he already had his pencil and notebook in hand.

But the person he noticed most was Larson. He was whispering something to his assistant as the judge pounded the gavel to begin the proceedings. However, what caught Joe's eyes mostly was the tie Larson was wearing. It was a bow tie—a bright red bow tie.

As the hearing began, judge Mandy read the defendant her rights under rules regarding non U.S. citizens accused of activity harmful to this nation and followed all the other procedures authorized by the international court of law. Kavinsky stifled a yawn and nearly fell asleep until hearing Larson give his opening arguments for the defense.

The man was smooth indeed, thought Joe, as he watched him go gracefully right into the issues and apparently win the attention and friendship of those present. It was obvious to Kavinsky why he was regarded so highly among some of his peers.

That's why it was so surprising that Larson, following his opening presentation, switched all of a sudden to portraying Salid as being weak-minded for being lured into joining the terrorist gang she was with when arrested. He also totally avoided any mention of her plea bargain. However, the biggest surprise came when he concluded by saying: "And, I admit judge, that it's very difficult to justify what she is accused of, considering that the group she tied in with was notorious and determined to kill Americans. This may be acceptable in her country—and perhaps she should go there."

If he's trying to defend her by describing her as an idiot he's doing a great job so far, thought Joe who began squirming on the hard courtroom seat wondering about the reason for this strange change of strategy on the lawyer's part. He also wondered what others might be thinking and looked about to see their expressions. But when he looked at Leo he found the young attorney sternly looking back at him.

Leo, too, had a frown on his face as though wondering what the hell was going on. Moreover, Al already was also gazing at Joe to find out what his nephew thought of this negative presentation to the hearing panelists who were selected, or almost hand-picked, by Mandy and others connected with the U.S. Attorney's Office.

More curiosity was heard when the judge called a recess and Kavinsky, Benjamin and Morrison got a chance to get together in the hallway for a discussion of the proceedings thus far.

"I admit, it's very unusual Joe for a defense attorney to try to win a case based on the naivetè of his client. But perhaps Ralph's strategy is to first emphasize the innocence of this woman compared to the scheming, treacherous gang she was with."

"Yeah—Joey. He probably wants to point out how she was duped into all this," explained Al who added, "but this sure makes her look stupid."

The words "probably" and "perhaps" clung to Kavinsky's mind as he still considered Larson's remarks that nearly bordered on an insanity plea. She didn't need that, he thought. She was not ignorant as Larson would have those present believe but very capable of knowing what she was doing, as evidenced by leading authorities who were helped by Salid in capturing the Beck gang. Plus, she also was granted a written substantiated plea—accepted by top authorities in the presence of Joe.

Almost reading Joe's mind, Leo took him aside and nearly whispered: "Mr. Kavinsky I think you may want to give testimony as a witness if at all possible—especially if the defense gets too weak. After all, you were very close to what's going on and your remarks should be quite admissible."

Joe kept thinking about Leo's advice upon his return to the courtroom. It was quite obvious that as of now Larson was avoiding anything making Salid look good, and her plea bargain was definitely being sidetracked. When Larson sat down after his initial presentation, another attorney got up. He presumably was the lawyer appointed for the prosecution. After a warm welcome to those present he immediately took advantage of the defense attorney's rather cold reversal in citing the accused for not knowing what she was involved with by joining the terrorists.

Kavinsky could almost predict what the prosecutor would say next and wasn't surprised when he heard:

"Ignorance of the laws, my friends, whether it be U.S. or elsewhere, is no excuse for criminal action."

These somewhat petty words came from the large but highly respected mouth of Peter J. Letsen, head of the prestigious law firm of Letsen, Pagel & Ordwell apparently recently named as the official prosecuting team. Joe's first reaction was that it didn't take Letsen's impressive credentials to mouth such a simple saying. But he knew where it was heading.

Judging from the smiles on the faces of Letsen's partners, each with large briefcases at their side, things were headed very much in the right direction—and at this point at least there was no need to even bring up anything relating to a plea bargain.

Why Letsen thought it necessary to have his partners sit in on this case, which would usually be considered almost routine for him, was well understood by both Joe and Al. The amount of press on hand nearly filled the courtroom, with some of the media standing near the doors unable to find any sitting room. What a great publicity opportunity for the lawyers involved, thought Al.

Oddly enough, even the judge seemed okay with the media attention. Mandy was known to usually "hate" the press. Most of the media just shrugged this off, knowing he objected to anything that would make his cases extra long—after all they figured, the shorter they are the more time he has for his beloved golf. They smirked over his heresy.

Joe and his uncle also knew that this was a very special case, one which would enable the judge and legal prosecutors to make extra headlines by showing their support to bring quick justice to anyone suspected of anything dealing with terrorism. The question of plea bargaining with such a suspect would certainly be looked down on by many of his influential and affluent friends.

Letsen declared, "Your honor, the whole terrorist scenario that took place at our famous mall and clinic was conducted with the help of this woman. To say she helped in any way to interfere with their evil plans is as much a fabrication of truth as saying the World Trade Center buildings were not destroyed by terrorists. She sits here today, brazen enough to wear her veil and robe, expecting us to be as gullible as she was just described so aptly by her defense attorney."

With that Larson, expected to frown at this reference, instead smiled somewhat as though in agreement with Letsen's attack on his client. He wrote something down on his legal pad, but Joe felt this was merely for show—pretending to counter with an argument.

Leo was sitting in the back of the chamber frowning over what he was hearing or seeing. Nameed also could be seen, staring intently—but mostly at Larson. It was as though he was also greatly upset that Ralph wasn't already up on his feet objecting to the prosecution's negative portrayal of Salid.

The judge finally rapped for a recess, then beckoned the lawyers into his chambers. As usual, Mandy's face didn't reveal if he was pleased or irritated with how the proceedings were beginning. He wanted to be as objective in his cases as possible. But both lawyers could notice a slight indication of a smile and in so doing got a message that they were doing a good job thus far. The question was: who was doing the best?

Mandy didn't mince words. He complimented them both, noting that they all seem to agree that the Muslim woman prisoner was indeed an accomplice in this act of terrorism. He appeared very relieved that there would be no great arguments to cause any delays in this already highly publicized court drama.

"Everything seems to be going along fine, gentlemen. I must say, however, that when the plea bargain issue comes up there may be some strong discussion and arguments. I assume you both are prepared for this?"

"Perhaps we can go light on this, judge, or even ignore it. After all, she isn't a citizen and it's not like her rights as such are being violated," noted Larson.

The judge sat back and grinned, saying "I'm rather surprised at you Ralph. You must have a real master plan to defend her if you're not emphasizing the plea bargain."

"You know me judge—she'll get the defense she has coming," replied Larson grinning back.

"You're making my job rather easy Ralph," joined in Letsen. "I'm sure the media is eating this up."

"You can be assured I'll be giving you a fight Peter," warned Larson. "I'm convinced of that Ralph. But you and I both know from experience that when you have someone pinned down at the beginning it's usually twice as hard to get them up again as a winner."

"You've been watching too many wrestling matches," remarked Larson with a snarl-type grin.

With that, the judge interrupted the haranguing by having his bailiff pour coffee and those attending touched their cups together as in a toast of goodwill.

As this was going on, Joe and his uncle also had a chance to convene and talk more about Dana Goodwin's escape, and where she might be hiding. They knew the DEA was busy, and silently, searching for her in hope of preventing her from harming the woman she was seen stalking at the spring break festival…the agent who Goodwin apparently felt had been getting in the way of her romance with Paulson.

"How can Terry be sure Dave and Dana were lovers?" asked Al, as he and Joe tried to avoid being bumped into by the large crowd of reporters also waiting for the strange case to resume. "Just remember unc, this has to be very confidential. If a story breaks on this the DEA hunt could be futile," reminded Joe looking about at the variety of media buzzing around them.

"However, Johnson said the DEA has found evidence of this—both on Dave and papers left behind at their office by Dana. Seems they were loving it up for some time behind the scene."

"Yeah, but how did the other agent get involved?" asked Al.

"According to Terry, Dana was so infuriated over this she even scribbled vicious notes to her rival, warning her to stay away from Paulson. The notes were found in checking her apartment and office locker."

Al, shrugging, said, "And the name of this other lover was on the notes, right?" Joe responded, "I only know what the DEA is telling me unc. This is their case—and their job. God knows I have enough to take care of," said Joe checking his watch to make sure they aren't late for the opening of the next session."

Before the court doors opened again, he added, "I also know Terry was quite pleased with your help in tracing down where these shady ladies may be in sunny Florida. He has a crew of agents already there in hope of catching up to them."

Upon entering the courtroom again, they spotted Leo waiving to them to join up with him. Sitting next to Joe gave Leo another chance to encourage Kavinsky to testify about the plea contract.

"The way this is going, Joe, I wouldn't be surprised if Salid is railroaded back home," he almost whispered.

"Maybe I should let my buddies in the press know about this so-called plea Joey?" offered his uncle overhearing what Leo was saying.

"No, not yet. I should first check with chief Hermes and Terry about this. As you know, they were with me when the plea bargain was made. It's better that way—it will have more clout," explained Joe.

"You'd better do this soon, Mr. Kavinsky," advised Leo. "I sense that even the judge wants to close the case as fast as possible and get rid of all the crowd and attention. In some ways, Mandy's a very shy guy."

As these words were said, the DEA special undercover team was busy figuring out where their traitor agent was hanging out. They began first by visiting with Tyrone of AP Wire-Photo. He still had the picture release forms filled out by some of those in the photo to give them. Unfortunately, there were no signatures of Dana but there was of the other agent, Gloria Marks. The scenario Johnson imagined, was that Gloria was the first to go to Miami, innocently ignoring a trail via a memo to her fellow workers about her vacation plans that made it quite easy for Dana to follow her.

The DEA knew that Gloria was a single mom with a teenage son who loved the excitement and wild fun of spring breaks. Terry guessed she traveled to Florida to observe some of this excitement, little knowing that she was also being observed by the mad and vengeful Goodwin.

The agents, by way of school records disclosing where Gloria's son was staying in the beach area, were able to talk with him and find his mom. She was just drying off after a plunge in the roaring ocean when encountered by her covert fellow agents.

Gloria appeared quite startled when told that Goodwin had also been following her and was embarrassed while admitting her secret romance with Paulson. One of the reasons for taking off so suddenly to Florida was her attempt to forget Dave's sudden death, she explained.

Did she know that Dana was so wildly infatuated with Dave? Did she indicate she wanted no competition and could even be a raging, jealous control-freak when it came to loving him?

Gloria answered no to both questions.

"I had other interests, and I thought Dana did also. I must say Dave led both of us on, as well as others. He was even trying to squeeze in some love affair with that girlfriend of Amad—what's-his-name."

"Turkos—Amad Turkos," one of the interrogating agents responded.

"He's dead, too," another agent added.

"I know, it's a murderous circle Dave got involved with. It didn't really surprise me that he ended up the way he did. I had to get away from it all as quickly as possible and my son's upcoming break gave me a nice break from it."

"Apparently, you had no idea Dana was also fleeing away."

"None whatsoever. Nor did I have any idea she was anywhere near the area where that picture you showed me was taken."

"Did you have any suspicion that she may have killed him?"

"I'm shocked over your thinking that she may be involved, but now that you told me, I can see her becoming so enraged with him."

"And with you, perhaps?"

"Perhaps. But had I known of her intense feelings for him I most certainly would have backed off."

"Do you know she may be stalking you?"

"Not until now. Frankly, I'm scared—knowing how she could do this quite well."

The head agent offered some advice and encouragement, however. "Knowing you may be her next target could enable us to catch her before she does any more harm." He then discussed a plan that, hopefully, might ensnare this crafty female so experienced in ensnaring others.

As this was happening, Joe and his uncle wondered how to be crafty enough to protect Salid from what they thought was unfair trial proceedings. Like Gloria, they welcomed some professional advice and Leo was pleased to offer it.

"I thought our justice system must always conform to what you lawyers call 'Due Process of the Law,'" Kavinsky noted while talking to Morrison.

"Yes, and in most cases it does. But this case involves so many other variables that I'm not sure the process will be followed according to the letter of the law."

The detective pondered this response for several minutes and then, looking at Leo said seriously, "You know, in a way, this sort of relates to the Holy Days, even to the site where Christianity is said to began."

"What do you mean Joe?" asked his uncle.

"I mean the way Salid is being treated. She's originally not too far from biblical country. Indeed, her promise of a plea bargain may be ignored by way of betrayal like it was done in the Bible—for 30 pieces of silver."

Leo nodded in agreement, saying "Yeah, like the apostles—everyone around asked: 'Is it I Lord?' Even the traitor Judas."

The banging of the judge's gavel brought them back abruptly to the present.

"Hear yee, hear yee!" announced the bailiff, "the court has now resumed."

CHAPTER 13

Joe's little group of Salid boosters hung around until the opening-day hearing was concluded. They knew there may be lots more drama yet to come, and perhaps just as tough on the defendant…even more so. Indeed, some of those attending seemed to be shaking their heads negatively as they departed following the description of Salid and her reported role in this scenario.

In observing this, Leo took Joe by the arm and reminded him, "You see what I mean, you must make sure that you get the chance to be a witness. Everyone seems to be intentionally avoiding this."

He added somewhat dramatically, "Think of the Good Book Joe. The defending lawyer is like Judas, perhaps he's even given her a kiss as a phony friend. But in my book it seems like he's leading her directly to her enemies waiting to kill her."

With Leo's words still in mind, Kavinsky made it a point to quickly contact chief Hermes and Johnson to update them on how the hearing was going. He considered this an urgent priority over all the other projects he faced that day.

"But we have to get permission from our bosses, Joe," noted Terry, as Hermes nodded in agreement regarding their involvement in testifying."

"And who might that be?"

"Although it's an Attorney General matter, in our case it has to come from our leaders at the DEA and, I'll bet, even from the mayor office for the chief."

"Is that possible?"

"Possible, but perhaps not probable."

"Home Security also may be involved. In a way, this is one of that department's primary duties—to assure resistance against any form of terrorism on the home front and encourage the revealing and combatting of any attempted terror attacks."

"Sounds very complicated and time-consuming," said Joe.

After a pause as the trio thought more about such strategy, the chief came up with another possible plan. "What say we try getting to the judge. After all Mandy has been so one-sided on anything catering to liberals he'd probably welcome some publicity on being moderate and fair-minded, at least to the extent of giving everyone an equal chance to explain why they're on the side of the accused."

"Who do we select to approach him about this?" Hermes asked.

"Anyone representing a multitude of readers, who, of course, are also voters," Johnson responded, knowing Mandy's desire for good publicity that might focus on his broad-minded judgement, rather than always a conservative hardliner.

Joe immediately snapped his fingers. "I've got it—why not my uncle Al? I'm sure the judge often reads his articles and knows the paper has a very big circulation."

"There's so many reporters wanting to talk to the judge as it is, how can we single out one over the others without the entire media coming down on us?" questioned Hermes.

"Al knows Larson. He could help give him an entrée to the judge. He and Mandy both seem to think alike. Remember all those cases they sort of won together—so much so that you kinda wonder how palsy-walsy they really are. Besides, my uncle rather respects Ralph's skills and has written him up well in the past."

Joe added, "But seeing how Larson has handled this situation so far, my uncle has indicated to me that the defense isn't really getting a fair shake and the judge seems to be going along with it all."

Noting his uncle's objective track record as a police reporter and the respect and trust he's gained among his media peer group, Kavinsky assured Johnson and Hermes that Benjamin's fellow news reporters would gracefully accept the fact that Al was indeed deserving of a scoop by directly talking with the judge. Besides, noted Joe, they probably would like to avoid the tough talking judge.

But the question remained, will Mandy grant Al an interview? Al welcomed the challenge to find out. As a veteran newsman, he was acquainted with various strategies to gain favor even with the most high-and-mighty in order to obtain a specially difficult story. One of his favorite ways was to work on their egos, noting that the story being planned would make the interviewee look exceptionally good. Another way was to warn them—very subtly of course—that if they didn't come up with some answers their egos might very well be tarnished.

The real reason for the Mandy interview, however, was to let the judge know Al was officially informed of the special plea bargain that was accorded to Salid. Mandy would then know the word was out and he couldn't resist avoiding this any longer. Also, Al would attempt to find out if the judge would allow the people who witnessed the plea bargain promise to testify about this at the hearing.

"If not, why not"...Benjamin said to his nephew rhetorically as they walked down the many steps leading from the courthouse to the parking lot.

"I think he'll go along with it," said Joe. "There's pressure on him—and being a clever, intelligent man he'll know he's caught in a corrupt situation if he denies this and doesn't allow such witness-stand evidence to be introduced."

Kavinsky felt good about leaving it to his uncle to get the judge to agree to this. He knew Al, as a seeker of truth, was an expert at persuasion. In fact, he found time to go home on time to love his wife and baby Matilda. Sarah was surprised when he opened the door so early. She glanced at her watch to see if it had stopped.

After considerable hugging, all three began enjoying family life. Sarah's tasty lasagna, along with Zinfandel wine, was more than welcomed as well as the baby's playing with her food. Once the table was cleaned and the late evening news watched, they checked out the baby asleep in her crib, and then ventured into bed for some very serious and passionate love-making.

Sarah interrupted this romantic scene only once, when she got tangled up in the bed sheets.

"Did you notice our fancy new sheets?"

"How would I do that with both of us almost under them?"

"Well, I hope you like them. They sure did cost a lot."

"Oh?" said Joe, rising up for a second to check them out.

"A bed sheet's a bed sheet," he said quickly going back to embracing his lovely wife."

He added, between kisses, "I'm sure we can afford gold ones. In fact, we could afford more than two homes like this and several limousines."

"Oh Joe, we haven't that much money."

"Well, figure it out. Both you and your sister Susan each inherited a fortune from your daddy and it's now collecting interest. Suppose Saddam's palace is for sale?"

"Oh hush!—remember we promised not to mention this."

"Sure—but I don't think anyone can hear us under these sheets."

That said, they snuggled up to one another again and remained that way until the alarm clock and crying Matilda notified them that it was time to go to work again.

As Sarah described her need for a more updated microwave and oven, Joe finished off his favorite breakfast cereal and looked over his schedule for the day. After reminding her once more that they now had money to buy the best appliances available, he checked over his schedule. One project he had highlighted reminded him to check with his uncle to see what headway Al was making with cranky judge Mandy.

Al knocked gently on the judge's shiny oak doors. He had visited with judges before and they always quickly made him at ease and were willing to talk with him. The press badge Al was wearing, however, made him wonder how comfortable Mandy may feel in talking to a high profile reporter and responding to some specific questions Benjamin had prepared.

A pretty smiling secretary, however, gave Al a warm welcome, but said it would be a few minutes yet before the judge could see him. Looking around at the walls of the judge's chambers impressed Benjamin as he noticed the many affluent and influential big shots the judge was pictured with. Seems like he was shaking hands with about everyone but the Pope, thought Al.

A loud buzz distracted Al from his star-gazing as a loudspeaker beaming the judge's voice said: "All right Wilma, send Mr. Benjamin in—remind me however to call the Supreme Court in about ten minutes."

Al got the message very clearly. Mandy was only allowing a very brief visit with him. He felt his pockets to make sure his questions were readily available. Patting down the few hairs around his bald spot, Benjamin mustered up enough confidence to meet the unsmiling judge sitting behind a huge desk.

The judge didn't get up, nor did he stop writing on a pad next to his phone. Al thought he was as intimidating as his desk—solid and unbreakable. He knew immediately he might have a very difficult time, as short as it would be, to get the judge to acknowledge his questions.

"I've heard of you Mr. Benjamin—your credentials speak well of your journalistic abilities," said the judge pushing his note pad aside but still not rising to shake Al's waiting hand. "But if you're here to obtain information regarding the current media circus that's going on over that Muslim girl I'm afraid you'll have to take your turn with the many other reporters covering this event."

"I assure you judge that I'm not concerned about what's taken place. As noted in my request to talk with you, I'm more interested in preparing an article on a notable judge in our midst—namely you. You've done so much for so many who don't realize it. I know, for example, that you have kept much corruption, violent crimes and drug dealers away from our homes and streets by sending many of the perpetrators off to jail," Al said with his fingers crossed.

"Harrumph" was about all the judge could mutter, apparently puffed up by such flatter. "I admit I try to do my part in doing away with such liberal violators."

"Yes—and this is quite apparent in the present case you're judging."

Mandy sat back and lit a cigar. Blowing out as much smoke as hot air, he continued, "I won't allow terrorism or anything bordering on it to escape my justice, Al. You gotta come down hard on that and send them away to what they've got coming."

"I can see Salid is well on her way to that," Al butted in, taking advantage of the judge tapping off cigar ashes.

"And rightly so…the evidence seems overwhelming."

"But don't you think it might go the other way when her plea bargain is brought up?"

Mandy could only cough as cigar smoke bellowed from his mouth. Upon spitting in the spittoon next to his feet he said with a red face, "What do you mean plea bargain?—you must have been talking to some of those fanatics out there in the crowd."

"No—I heard this from some very reliable sources judge, including the DEA and local police."

"Well, you won't hear it in my courtroom, you can bet on that."

"But judge, wouldn't that be like withholding evidence? They maintain there was a legal promise made to this young lady if she would help lead authorities to the arrest of the terrorists in our mall and clinic."

Mandy was up on his feet by now, crushing out his cigar in the tray on his desk. "I can't understand why or how anyone could defend her when she admits to being part of their gang."

"But Larson's suppose to do that. After all he was assigned to be her defense attorney by your court."

"What are you suggesting? I understood this was suppose to be a feature on me instead of focusing on others—especially those bastards bent on terrorizing our country."

Al, sensing Mandy was getting out of control, wanted to quickly finish this conversation. "But Judge, aren't you going to allow authorities who promised the plea bargain a chance to explain their side as testimony? If you don't, won't that make you look bad—it certainly wouldn't lend credence to my article featuring you as being very objective. Besides, as I recall, the Mideast docs who tried to destroy DNA evidence linking the terrorist leader at our big medical clinic were also granted a plea bargain for their disclosure. It was quickly accepted by the court, unlike Salid's, isn't this unfair?"

Mandy stepped away from Benjamin, put his hand to his chin and seemed to be in deep thought pondering Al's latest remarks before saying, "I'll talk to the attorneys about this. They sometimes get too involved to see the big picture. Start your story and I'll have something to fill in about this," he assured the somewhat relieved Benjamin.

Joe assumed his uncle completed his visit with Mandy when he saw another Post-it-note on his phone later that morning. It was from Ralph Larson. Liz warned him that the voice on the phone sounded quite angry and wanted Joe to call him "ASAP". Before he could return this call, however, he was interrupted by another call, this time from Harim Nakeem.

Without getting the time to even say good morning, Joe heard some form of aerobic jabbering on the other end. Whatever it was, it also sounded upset. "Hey, calm down—we're in America, remember. Speak the language," urged an impatient Kavinsky accustomed to responding this way when talking to the growing number of foreigners moving to the Twin Cities, and encountering problems that hopefully the police can handle.

"I'm sorry, Mr. Kavinsky. For a moment I thought I was talking to another contact from the Mideast. This is Harry Nakeem—the lawyer sitting in on the Salid Ashton case. I am so troubled by how it is going that I must have misdialed and thought I was leaving word on my office voice-mail for my assistant who also is from my home town."

Accepting this apology, Joe probed more into why Nakeem felt the trial was not proceeding right.

"For one thing, I believe I was unfairly removed from defending Salid by Larson and the judge. It is not me they should have been suspicious of, Mr. Kavinsky, but Larson who in my opinion is out to get that poor girl."

"What makes you think that? I understand he has some great credentials as a criminal trial lawyer."

"Yes, but have you really researched his past? I mean years back when he was over in the Mideast himself."

"Can't say I have. What are you getting at Harim?"

There was a long pause on the other end until Nakeem finally said, "I can't go into this any more with you on the phone, Mr. Kavinsky. This is a matter we must discuss in great privacy. Can we meet in a place we will not be overheard in any way. Perhaps you as a detective can suggest such a meeting site...and please call me Harry."

The tone of Nakeem's voice sounded urgent enough that Joe immediately thumbed through his list of restaurants offering some sort of privacy and intimacy.

"There's a place over by River Road that's off the main drag and has booths providing extra privacy for conversation. I believe that should work out—if it's okay with you Harry."

"It should be fine. But we must do this soon since I believe the way this trial is going a sentence will be announced very soon."

Glancing at his watch again, Joe shook his head, looked at his schedule pad and then erased a rather sociable luncheon date with some of his precinct buddies. "How about this noon? The place is called The Hilltop—it's away from almost everything."

"That should be fine. I'll be alone and will bring along my research report on Mr. Larson. I'm sure you'll find it quite interesting."

As Joe jotted down the time and place of this meeting, chief Hermes tapped on his desk. "Gotta see you in my office...right away," he demanded.

When the chief closed his door after Joe entered, Kavinsky suspected that the conversation would be about the DEA since Hermes wanted any communication about their involvement with that agency and circumstances around Paulson's death kept very confidential between only Joe, the chief and Terry Johnson.

"While you were on the phone, Johnson called me and told me his DEA agent Dana is headed back to the Twin Cities," the chief announced immediately.

"But why in the world would she want to come back here when she's a suspect in Dave's death?" asked a confused Kavinsky.

"Johnson said he believes she's still stalking the agent who was dating Dave on the side. I guess she must want to get revenge so badly she's willing to risk being caught up here," explained the chief.

"Ah, sweet revenge. She sounds a little nuts," muttered Joe.

"Crazed is the word. Whatever was going on between Paulson and that other woman created a terrible triangle that eventually took Dave's life and may very well take the other woman's according to Johnson." Kavinsky asked, "does Terry have a fix on her, does she know where she is now?"

"I'm not sure. Remember Joe, she's also trained as a spy like Terry. She could be right next door. Our main link is to follow the woman she's after, you can bet that Dana's very nearby."

"Does the other woman—I believe her name is Gloria Marks—know about all this?"

"Terry said he purposely called her back to the DEA office here thinking Dana may want to follow her undercover. Keep in mind, Dana is hopefully still not aware that she's a suspect. As you'll recall, the DNA research was done very secretly in finding out who shoved that knife into Dave."

The chief added, "as to whether Gloria knows the danger she's in, a little—but not enough to upset any plans to snatch her pursuer. Dana, I'm sure, still has pals and associates around these parts who might tip her off."

"If Terry's setting them up for a showdown, where and when do you think this will happen?"

"Dunno yet. I suggest you get in touch with Terry to give you the latest update on this."

Joe, however, wasn't in a big hurry to check further into this strange scenario involving these DEA women. His mind was more on how to help the apparently mistreated lady in the federal lockup awaiting appearance before biased Judge Mandy. In fact, he left his precinct in mid morning to visit once again with Salid to see for himself how she was getting along amid all the judicial and seemingly sinister problems she was facing.

Expecting a lonely and depressed prisoner, Kavinsky instead encountered two smiling Mideast ladies welcoming him into her cell. One was the prisoner who seemed to brighten up considerably when Joe appeared and the other was her sister who resembled Salid not only in expression….but good looks.

"My sister came to cheer me up, and now I have two very nice friends to do so," said Salid welcoming the quizzical detective. "I am sometimes called naïve in choosing my friends, many have been bad and untrustworthy, but I know for sure both of you are here to help me."

Joe took this opening regarding true friendship to ask, "do you consider your lawyer to be a friend?"

"No, I believe he is making a case against me. Why is he not mentioning the plea bargain I was granted instead of making me look demented?"

"I'm not sure. But I think we'll have our day in court to go over all this, even though the judge may try to avoid it."

"With the grace of God this will be treated fairly," counseled Paola holding a rosary. Joe was then surprised when both got down on the floor, the Christian on her knees and the Muslim bent over with her head on a tiny rug.

Kavinsky just stood there in awe, hearing both in prayer. Paola beseeching Jesus the saviour and Salid the almighty Allah. Although not being a very religious fella, Joe lowered his head and whispered, "please Lord, let there be justice."

Upon being reassured by the jailers present that the prisoner was receiving proper treatment, Kavinsky returned to the precinct uplifted somewhat by what he witnessed but still wondering when Salid would receive her hearing in court. The jailers let him know that her defense lawyer seldom visited her and when he did he seemed to be angry and not providing advice.

With all this in mind, he nearly forgot he had a noon meeting with lawyer Nakeem at the Hilltop. He shuffled his paperwork aside, noticing that the Northside drug business was slowing down, reached for a paper and pen to take notes, and hustled off to the restaurant to talk to this rather unknown attorney who seemed to know so much about his competitor Larson. He also wondered if either one could really be trusted.

In driving to the restaurant he realized why it was called the Hilltop. It seemed like he would never reach the summit of the rough and winding road he was on. It was even tougher to drive than usual with all the repair work being done with the arrival of Spring. Winter, of course, left its usual toll of numerous pot holes.

When he arrived, a middle-aged man with a cap pulled down almost to his eyebrows was at the door with a slight smile. At first Joe thought this might be the restaurant manager until the dark-skinned greeter said, "Hello Mr. Kavinsky I've been looking forward to meeting you for some time."

"Are you Nakeem?" asked a somewhat startled Joe.

"Please, as you'll recall, I go by Harry. Although I was born in the Mideast and am a Muslim I prefer being referred to by a good old fashion USA name."

This opening somewhat took the edge off their introduction to one another. As they found a secluded booth both were smiling and apparently looking forward to their upcoming but unpredictable conversation.

Even before a waiter came around to take their order, this dark-skinned man with piercing eyes began talking seriously. "Joe—and I hope I can call you that for surely Salid does in fond admiration—I must inform you about that man who is supposed to be defending her. Unlike me, he was born and raised in America but unlike me he is more a replica of the harsh fundamental Islamic side of my country."

"How can that be?" interrupted Kavinsky gazing up from the menu handed to him by the waiter who left to get some coffee requested by the new arrivals.

"He is a rich man to begin with. In fact, his father is still quite wealthy and was able to take his young son to Pakistan on one of his international lawyer conferences. While there I am told Ralph met up with students from Islamic schools who were attempting to form a united Islamic state. Like his father, Ralph—his real name is Raldo—was scholarly and eager to absorb information he could about this group."

"What's it called?" asked Joe looking up from his menu.

"The Taliban, which is also spelled taleban, meaning seekers after knowledge."

Nakeem continued, "It was formed in 1994. The group wanted to end the lawlessness and suffering that resulted from years of civil war in Afghanistan and drew some of their forces from Afghan and Pakistani Muslim students."

"But how does this relate to Larson?"

"He was so influenced by the group that when he returned to this country he learned more about it and wanted to join up with them. However, his father wouldn't allow this and Ralph had to be in contact with them behind the scenes."

"How do you know all this?"

"Being from that part of the world, I have many friends who have kept me well informed."

Taking a sip from the glass of water brought first by the waiter, Joe sat back, frowned, and asked his most direct question: "Are you trying to tell me that Larson is being paid off by the Taliban?"

"Exactly. They want desperately to punish that woman severely."

"How do I know you're telling me the truth?"

"Trust me, Mr. Kavinsky. Check my record as a good and capable lawyer. With the terrorism around us, I'm afraid I have become unfairly profiled at times as a suspect simply by my appearance and perhaps mannerism, but my resume speaks for itself. I fled the turmoil of the Mideast years ago to live in a more gentle, civilized nation. I found what I was seeking in America, and fondly hold it in my heart and with the utmost respect. Believe me, I would do nothing to harm this nation and greatly appreciate its regard for human life and fair treatment to its people."

"And this is why you're protecting Salid?"

"Yes. I can see through Larson and know where he's coming from—although some think he is bright, I think he is shady and deceitful."

For a moment, neither man spoke. Nor did they consume any food on the table, but seemingly were digesting every word that had been spoken. To break the somewhat eerie silence, Joe asked Nakeem if it was okay to smoke in this offbeat restaurant. Given a nod by his companion, he lit a cigarette and blew out the smoke while further considering what was said about Larson.

He then asked, "What about Letsen—good guy or bad?"

Nakeem hesitated with his response as though giving this considerable throught. A little too long, perhaps, thought Joe.

"Peter is a good attorney, but a little too zealous and ambitious to please the judge. Both he and Mandy, in my opinion, wish to make headlines by showing utter contempt for all those daring to undermine the nation, although the judge pretends he is impartial—he really is a racist in many ways."

"Boy, those are harsh words Harry," Kavinsky said snuffing out his cigarette.

"Yes, but very true. I am convinced Letsen would do anything he believes the judge wants just to play up to him."

After further digesting all this negative input, Joe finished off his lunch and checked his watch to discreetly let Nakeem know he needed to return to the police precinct. "I'll sure keep all this in mind Harry, and you can be certain I won't disclose anything you've told me to anyone."

"I know you are trustworthy. And I also know you have an uncle who is a popular newspaper writer. Perhaps there is some way you can transfer my concerns about Larson to him that will help Salid in her desire for the treatment she has been promised." Kavinsky was glad to hear that, knowing he and Al already were questioning the unusual and negative way Salid was being defended.

Before departing, the detective asked—as though wanting to get something off his chest—"As a close observer of how this case is going, Harry, do you think I should speak out as a witness to the plea bargain made in my presence—as well as in the presence of the DEA and police chief?"

Nakeem smiled and without hesitation replied, "Yes, there is no doubt about it, you and the others who heard this. I am sure the judge and Larson have already conspired to keep this from happening, however. But it must be done, and done as soon as possible." The detective remarked, "Thanks Harry—Seems you've done your homework."

With Nakeem's final words of advice still in mind, Joe headed back to his desk to tackle once again the many projects piling up. During the entire time driving the busy freeway he kept wondering how his uncle was doing convincing Mandy to allow such witness testimonial.

His answer was indicated on a note posted on his office phone. His secretary Liz simply scribbled: *"Call your uncle—said thing's are okay."*

Joe pushed aside the other papers on his desk and quickly called Al at the newspaper office. However, he was told that his uncle was in a conference with the editor at the time. Joe was about to leave a message on Al's voice-mail when Benjamin cut in with "Hey Joey, what's up? Did you get my note?"

"Sure did—sounds like you were successful in getting the judge to say okay. But I hope you didn't say anything about this to your boss."

"Don't worry, it's all still very confidential. Mandy is still shaking, thinking about what would happen to his reputation if word gets out on the possibility of his even thinking about withholding such eye-witness information."

"Good unc. I take it then that Terry, the chief, and I can expect to be called to the stand soon," Al said, "it could be as early as his next session Joe."

"Great job unc. I'll let the others know immediately and we'll be prepared to be grilled on this subject." Upon hanging up, the phone rang almost immediately again. This time his ID caller showed it was from his wife. "Sorry honey, but I'm really rushed. Al's given me information—that I gotta call Terry about right away," was Joe's opener.

"Sounds like you've hit the panick button," responded Sarah. "But I guess there's no hurry about this. I just wanted you to know that I got a voice-mail for you at the house—it was from a Gloria. Do you know a Gloria? She just said to call her as soon as possible." Joe asked, "Did you get her last name?"

"It sounded like Mark—or Marks. She seemed nervous. Even a little scared."

"Hmm, I might know her—but we've never met. This seems more like a matter for Johnson. I'll get in touch with him pronto. Thanks for the call—love ya…and give my love also to Matilda," said Joe as he wondered what the baby may be flinging now to the pup from her high chair.

Once again, Kavinsky considered tossing a coin in the air to figure out what to do next. He realized Johnson and Hermes should be quickly told about testifying to Salid's plea, but he also knew it was important to sound an alert about Gloria Marks' call.

CHAPTER 14

❦

Joe figured he could cover two bases with a single call to Terry, one regarding his talks with Nakeem and Al and the other enabling him to ask Terry why Gloria Marks would be phoning him. The latter should be done before trying to return her call, he reasoned.

Regardless of how logical this seemed, Kavinsky also realized the chief's office was only a short walking distance away. What's more, Hermes was in his office for a change and apparently had no visitors.

The chief, as usual, stopped what he was doing when Joe knocked on his door. He always seemed to have time for the detective who was sort of regarded with pride around the precinct for his brave achievements. He had mixed feelings, however, upon hearing that Joe's uncle, the reporter, was able to convince the judge that he should have a special hearing from the actual witnesses to the plea.

"It's so damn controversial Joe. In a way, some might regard it as helping terrorism."

"But you know yourself chief what we promised this woman if she would lead us to those killers."

"Yes, but what if Home Security or other authorities find issue with that?. We'll be the ones in the headlines—maybe as much as the bad guys."

Surprised by such resistance, Joe scratched his head for a moment trying to explain this better. He then pointed out, "But there'll be three of us testifying to the same thing—supporting one another that this indeed was what Salid was promised in good faith. You won't be alone."

"Let me think about it. I know this has to be done soon. I'll get back to you tomorrow after sleeping on it," said Hermes rising from his chair indicating the conversation was closed for the time being.

That wasn't quite good enough for Joe who returned to his desk and began dialing Johnson. All he could get, however, was Terry's voice-mail requesting the caller to leave a message. Following DEA code regulations when calling an agent, he simply said *"TJ THIS IS JOKE—CALL BACK URGENT"* No matter how serious the matter involved might be, however, he always felt like chuckling knowing that JOKE stood for Joe Kavinsky and that TJ was Terry Johnson.

As soon as he began checking out another drug smuggling report his phone rang. He knew by the monitor that it was Terry. "My gosh, man, how did you get back so fast…you must have been sitting on the phone," kidded Joe.

"No way. I knew by the way the phone rang that you were in trouble again," replied his DEA buddy. Now what are you up to JOKE?"

"Just why the hell is Gloria Marks calling me at home?"

There was a pause as though Johnson needed time to answer. When he did there was no trace of any more teasing. "I can't answer that entirely. All I know is that she has no idea that we're using her to lure Dana back to us."

He continued, "I did tell her she's needed back here because of a murder investigation she's been involved with, and that it recently took on a new twist which calls for her personal attention. She got your name because I told her you were working with me on the case as a local police undercover. I suppose she simply looked you up in the phone book to talk about this. Sorry, I didn't figure she would do anything before first checking with our office."

"Don't bawl her out too much Terry, after all you interrupted her vacation and she should be a little irritated," responded Joe. "Maybe, too, the Associated Press could have told her my uncle was asking about that newspaper picture he spotted those two gals in."

Terry shrugged this off with a "whatever." But he warned once more, "just remember, don't let Gloria know we're using her to catch Goodwin."

"My—oh—my, the sneaky games you DEA guys play, even with one another," remarked Joe who was almost ready to hang up when he remembered the second reason for calling his DEA buddy.

"But we've got another problem Terry, one which could be even bigger than the Dana one. Seems my uncle was able to get the judge to allow us to take the witness stand, so to speak, testifying that Salid was granted a plea bargain in writing for her role in capturing Beck the terrorist. But chief Hermes seems hesitant to do this for fear of the after-effects which he indicated could be very controversial of course and perhaps jeopardize his position." Joe expected another pause as he ran this by Johnson for his thoughts on the subject. However, his reply came almost immediately. "What's fair is fair," declared Terry. "You can't have it two ways. All three of us heard the plea promise in the chief's office. She was good enough to help us every way she could at the risk of being mercilessly killed by that cold-hearted bunch. I'll call the chief and tell him that, and do all I can with DEA support to convince him to go along with this. After all, he's got this in writing...just like a contract."

"Whew," was about all Joe could mutter after clicking off. He was more than ready to go home to forget the bad times he may be facing and play with the baby and make love to his wife. But at about the same time, Sarah and Matilda were getting ready to have a good time at the giant mall in the nearby suburb; to stroll around and perhaps purchse some of the various items featured in the mall's highly promoted biggest sale of the year. Although she realized she now didn't need to worry about money due to her recent large inheritance, she even participated with numerous bargain hunters in signing up at a counter near one of the stores for a free family trip to Cancun. Lots of shoppers were bumping into one another to do likewise.

However, many bad memories still remained in Sarah's mind even though she was distracted by some very attractive merchandise for both her and Matilda, including a few toys. For one thing, she found herself in the same area where the terrorists set off a fire-alarm to begin their raid on the mall. She recalled that if it wasn't for that young veiled Muslim woman their plans for murder and destruction would have happened and that gang of killers would have gotten away.

She also thought how petty and naïve she must have been to get upset over that woman's secret calls to her husband regarding this matter. Sarah was inwardly scolding herself when she was suddenly nudged by another shopper. Although she was holding some packages, the nudger took time to say, "excuse me. but aren't you Mrs. Joe Kavinsky?"

Acknowledging that she was, the woman who bumped into her responded, "I'm Gloria—Gloria Marks."

"I'm sorry, but do I know you?" inquired Sarah surprised by this woman's sudden friendly greeting.

"Not really. I was in back of you when you registered for that free trip and noticed your name. I hope you win, I just returned from Florida and have too much sun as it is."

She continued, "I've been trying to reach your husband lately on some business matter. Could you give him a little note...if he can't get to me by phone I'll also give him my fax number and e-mail address."

As she was writing this out Sarah was looking around to see if she could spot that cute little blouse she saw in the store window. But she was interrupted in her store gazing quickly upon receiving the scribbled note from the rather tall, middle-aged looking woman. "Thanks for passing this on to your husband."

"Sure Gloria, I'll be certain to do that. Are you a cop, too?"

"In a way, in a special way I'd guess you'd say," she replied looking at her watch as if in a hurry to leave. "I'll be looking forward to hearing from Joe."

Sarah relayed this message on soon after her husband arrived home. "She says she's something special, do you know what that is?" asked the curious wife.

"Yeah—she's special all right—a special agent for the DEA. I can't believe that this was just an accidental meeting. Nothing is accidental with those super snoops."

"Well, she was all alone and very nice."

"Are you sure she wasn't with someone?"

"Not that I could notice, but there was such a crowd mingling around."

"Did you look about?"

"A little, but why do you ask?"

Without replying, Joe got up and headed for his old newspaper rack. He returned with an issue of the Tribune. With his wife wondering what he was up to, he unfolded the rather old paper and spread one page out on the kitchen table.

"Now look real hard Sarah. Do you recognize anyone in this picture?"

His wife looked inquisitively at Joe and then peered down at the photo on the page. She didn't say anything for awhile until thoroughly studying the photo and the caption describing the spring break taking place.

"Yes, that's the person I met at the mall...the one with the big red hat."

"Do you recognize anyone else, anyone in the background?"

Pausing, Sarah then exclaimed, You know honey, I think I might have seen someone else. She was way in the back of the crowd—yes, that's her!" Sarah said excitingly suddenly pointing to one of the onlookers watching the spring breakers celebrate.

"Her who?"

"That lady standing with the others near the resort. Look, she's also in your old newspaper photo."

"Are you absolutely positive that's who you saw?"

"Yes," she said with her hands on her hips. "You make me feel like I'm a victim checking out suspects lined up against a wall."

"You're not too wrong about that. If she's who I think, we might be looking at a real terrible suspect who, if not caught, could have many victims."

"And who might that be?—I don't know either of these woman you may be talking about."

"And I'm glad about that," Joe said hugging his wife.

He added, "I can't tell you much about this right now, but hopefully the one you recalled in this photo with that big hat is being looked at in the background by a very sinister gal who may be stalking her."

"You mean, she didn't follow me home?," kidded Sarah.

"Nope, she's probably too busy following the other gal…the one you were talking with after signing up for that special trip.

"How can you keep all your women straight," Sarah continued to tease. "First it was that one in the mall who called you so much, and now it's two others who seem to capture your attention."

"Now honey, duty is duty—it's not fun chasing after women," Joe kidded back.

"But just remember if you see either one again give me a quick call. This is a serious matter and you'd be at risk getting in the middle with these two."

Johnson was as excited as Joe when he was told about Sarah's brief encounter with Gloria and spotting Dana almost hiding near Gloria in the same photo—Terry considered Dana treacherous and Marks innocent but quite vulnerable.

"Why not have Gloria Marks visit your office, Terry? Hell, Dana Goodwin may just follow her right to your desk," Joe said chuckling. "You're living up to your code name, JOKE," warned his DEA pal sarcastically. "We can't let Dana know we're on to her."

"Yeah—but wouldn't it only be fair to let Gloria know? She's a sitting duck, Terry. I can't understand why she shouldn't be brought into this—for her own defense and safety."

"Maybe you're right Joe. I'll talk to my boss. He felt like I did at first—that by not telling her, Gloria would act very normal about everything without alarming Dana. We want Dana—but realize that she's a damn good snoop and would be gone forever if she had any inclination at all that we're on to her."

"'Hell hath no fury like a woman scorned,' eh Terry?" shrugged Joe roughly recalling some scripture which he figured may help describe the hatred that must be driving Goodwin. "God only knows…but we've got to put a stop to it or else we might have one, or even two, dead DEA agents," summed up Johnson thinking about the murder of Paulson and the dagger in his back.

But being fair apparently wasn't in the mind of the defense attorney involved with the case of the other woman problem worrying Kavinsky. While his attention was currently on helping to protect Gloria from Dana, Joe kept wondering if Larson would be in the way of his being called to the stand to give Salid a fair trial despite efforts of Al and the DEA to persuade chief Hermes to go along with this.

He found out very soon. Joe had just returned to his precinct when he heard from Larson who was cursing and talking so fast and loud that he could barely be understood. "Hey Ralph, calm down, it's hard to know what you're saying. What's going on? I just got back from another assignment."

He could almost hear Larson sputtering. "What the hell are you up to Kavinsky? I told you to stay out of this case and let me handle it. I don't want you testifying. Do you understand, am I making myself clear now?" This guy surely has guts but no class, thought the surprised detective. To help calm him down he tried putting him down.

"Is this the way you handle your clients, too? You may be able to bluff some of those women you handle Ralph, but you sure as hell aren't pushing me around."

"What women? Are you prying into my affairs again?"

"I heard about your shouting matches with that little Muslim girl in the detention cell."

This further incensed the arrogant lawyer. "You mean you've been visiting with her and going around me without my permission?"

"Since when does a cop have to have your permission for anything? especially one who apparently doesn't belong there in the first place."

"Do you know who you're dealing with?—I could bring you before the Supreme Court if I chose."

"Cool it Ralph. You must admit that you looked more like a prosecutor than a defense attorney at her hearing. Not once have you ever mentioned the plea bargain she was granted."

"Let me do my own form of defense Kavinsky. You stick to your business and I'll do mine, which I was so well educated to do in law school and during years of professional experience. I dare say as a cop, you probably haven't got many scholastic achievements to boast about."

Aware that Larson was a bit out of control and getting nasty, Joe stopped him immediately from getting too far out by asking: And where did you learn your technique Ralph?—was it from some Afghanistan or Pakistani teachers?"

Larson was speechless for a moment as though Joe hit a nerve with his remarks about Ralph's past. When he did respond his voice was calmer and gentler. He concluded by saying "Well Mr. Kavinsky, I'm sorry I got so upset. I'm sure we're both gentlemen and can forget and forgive. I do think it's important, though, that you stay out of my courtroom, let me do my thing and your girlfriend may get a break."

"Your courtroom, my girlfriend? What the hell are you insinuating Larson? As far as forgive and forget, I still think that young lady doesn't have a chance with you as her defender." With that, Joe slammed the phone down so hard that nearly everyone around the station could almost hear it striking the top of his desk.

Chief Hermes was passing by and stood near Joe frowning with his arms folded. "Wow, you sure get rough with those crooks you're after." he exclaimed.

"It wasn't a crook, but it might be a bad guy—a lawyer at that."

"Bad lawyers—boy you want to stay far away from them."

Joe, not wanting to spar around on the matter of Salid any longer, let him know directly what was said on the phone. "Chief we have to be plea witnesses or this girl will be deported and probably executed. We owe her justice!"

"You're right, your pal Johnson explained this to me further after we talked and I think it's only right that we tell the jury about our promise to her."

"Regardless of what the lawyers think? or those you report to? or what the public reaction is? or what this might do to a man in your position?" quizzed Joe. He answered, "Yes, regardless. You know, I do have a conscience and I remember distinctly the bargain we made with that woman. You, Terry and I were all there to hear it. Let's go forward with this in hope her plea discussion is at least heard by others."

"Great chief—and thanks!" said Joe rising to shake Hermes' hand. "She sure won't get any freedom if she's sent back to the Taliban." But his smile faded quickly, as he realized that if there was any way her clever defense attorney could prevent their testifying he was certainly going to use it to force her return to her native country.

CHAPTER 15

Moments before the courtroom opened for the next session of the Salid hearing Judge Mandy was still arguing with Larson in his private chamber about allowing anyone as a witness to testify to the plea bargain. He knew he was "out of order" since a one-sided partisan view, called "exparte" by attorneys, is frowned on if both lawyer sides aren't represented during such discussion with a judge.

"It would only confuse the matter. Besides what kind of authorities representing the law would offer such a plea?" Larson said almost waiving his hands. "We'd be better off not even bringing it up."

"I've gone over this often Ralph. But I think we can't prevent it. The press will hear, and it sure won't do anyone much good if we openly oppose it."

The judge, while removing his spectacles to make a point, said "I remind you that this is more a pre hearing—a bail hearing—rather than a downright trial and as a hearing all those involved should rightly be heard."

The judge then looked up at the disturbed Larson and added, "Besides Ralph, some are already wondering why you aren't making a better case for her." Before Larson could respond, a bailiff interrupted their discussion by reminding them that the hearing was ready to resume.

As both the judge and Larson entered the courtroom they could easily see Kavinsky, Johnson and Hermes sitting near the front row waiting for them. Benjamin also could be noticed with a pen and pad and a slight smile on his face.

All were asked to approach the bench as soon as the judge sat down. Larson, however, remained where he and the prosecutor attorney usually sit. As soon as all those were present before him, Mandy began to speak in a very low tone.

"You're aware that I have decided to take your testimony this morning regarding the alleged plea bargain of the accused. I have agreed to this. I would appreciate that you conduct yourselves in a manner reflecting the proper procedure of my court. Anyone not doing so will be ushered out of here," he said strictly.

They could tell that Mandy was extremely nervous and upset about all this. He was known as a rigid judge who, when he made up his mind about something, nothing would change it. That's why Al, although attempting to keep a very serious appearance, found it difficult not to grin a little.

The judge then tapped his gavel to let the hearing begin. He could only hope that this would not turn into what he called a "media circus." Al, on the other hand, hoped that his fellow reporters weren't miffed by his apparent conversations with the judge as evidenced by his being singled out for an exclusive interview with him.

It was apparent that no one cared if the prosecuting attorney was upset. Letsen frowned at the judge's pre-hearing conference while remaining seated with his hands crossed. His body language indicated his opposition. It was a slight he hadn't counted on, but immediately knew someone got to the judge to change his attitude and persuaded him to go along with the plea testimony.

The first plea witness was Johnson, who, after being sworn in, declared emphatically that a plea bargain had been granted to Salid, but has been ignored so far. The second, Hermes, described the meeting in his office and exactly when the plea discussion was made and federal authority given; and the third, Joe, not only reinforced what the others said, but also touched again on the many times the young woman risked informing authorities about the activities and whereabouts of the terrorist group.

Meanwhile Larson, who sat across from his competitor Letsen, looked tense and kept his mouth shut, although it was apparent he wanted to jump up and object. But as a veteran criminal defense lawyer, he knew this would be out of line and that he would be getting his chance to ask many questions following this testimony. He realized if there are no charges there would be no trial, allowing that woman loose without harsh punishment—not even public flogging as the Taliban would want.

He also knew he had to change his role of being an insensitive prosecutor to being a compassionate defender since the stage was changing somewhat and he was no longer getting the support expected from the judge.

The sudden change in Larson's tactics led to much discussion during the morning court break. Most of it was within the small group of Leo Morrison,

Joe and Al. "You've got the defense finally becoming the defender, as he should be," observed Leo. "It's so obvious that he couldn't defend himself against what was told by you and the others."

"Yeah, that guy can certainly turn it on and off," agreed Benjamin regarding the way Larson was starting to focus on Salid's efforts to help, rather than scoffing at her interference with those wishing to arrest the terrorist drug lord.

"Well, let's hope that continues. I'm not too convinced that it will," commented Joe. "He still may have something up his sleeves."

Their hallway conversation was cut short by the sudden jingling of Terry's cell phone. It was so loud that some of the press in the area stopped talking and taking notes. Terry withdrew to a corner away from the hallway and remained there for quite a few minutes. He seemed very serious and shook his head apparently surprised by what he was hearing.

"What's up old man?" asked Joe when his pal returned.

"Plenty—Gloria is back and may even be heading to this very courtroom, my office reports."

"But why? Doesn't she have anything else to do?"

"She's still on vacation Joe and may just be curious about all the attention this case is generating among the DEA," explained Johnson. "So look about gents, if you see any lady sitting here looking like Gloria be sure to get the word out."

With that, Terry showed the picture of her in Florida that was in the newspaper. As they looked around, thinking she could have arrived already, Leo nudged Joe and beckoned him aside as though wanting to whisper something to him.

"I've been thinking about what you said, wondering if Larson will really go all out to defend Salid. That worries me, too. You know, if she really wants to change attorneys at this point now is the time she may be able to."

"Really? I thought she was stuck with that guy and that she's bound for the Taliban," Joe said amazed.

"Not really—she still has the opportunity to do this under federal jurisdiction. That's not to say, however, that the judge might not interfere." Leo added, "And she may be spared from going back there because of a new ruling by the U.S. Attorney General's office that immigrants can now be detained from deportation if they have no ties to terrorism, in an effort to address broader security concerns. But I also understand the Board of Immigration Appeals has been slowing down in granting appeals to avoid deportation."

Although Kavinsky couldn't really understand all this "legalese", he smiled when seeing the grin on Leo's face indicating his great pleasure in outsmarting even the clever Larson.

"And even if you can't hold them indefinitely, this may provide a chance to come up with additional plans to keep her from the hands of the enemy," Leo noted.

"Sounds good," agreed Joe. "However, I sort of like your first point. If she can get an honest lawyer, like yourself, who can help her instead of the rather shifty one she now has…then I'd say let's try to do this."

Leo's expression indicated this would work. He then looked at Joe to make sure he heard correctly and Joe looked back confident of what he had said.

"How about it Leo, would you be her lawyer?"

Morrison blushed a little, like a kid being praised, and said "I'm still regarded as a rookie lawyer Joe, but I hate to see the law being violated like this. I'll be pleased to defend it by defending Salid the best way I know. But she has to hire me."

"And that's good enough for me," Kavinsky responded shaking Leo's hand. Joe and his young lawyer friend knew it wasn't going to be easy changing lawyers in the middle of this hearing, but they knew there would be some good support.

For instance, the judge himself even seemed to be questioning Larson's style. Moreover, the person he was supposed to defend disliked him and thought he was mishandling the case; and the DEA, and local police department represented by the chief and Joe, thought he was purposely withholding evidence that would greatly assist Salid.

Before the hearing could resume, Kavinsky and Leo were able to meet with Salid who agreed to switch to Leo. The judge was advised of this via proper channels and wasn't too surprised. He realized if that's what the accused wanted he was willing and even pleased to consider this, saying he would inform Ralph that he was now off the case. Leo figured Mandy was probably also relieved since this would be further indication that he wasn't as biased in his judgements as many thought him to be.

As they were walking away from the judge's chambers, Ralph was on his way there—as though curious as to why they were with Mandy. He almost scowled as he nearly bumped into Joe, indicating that he might know what was about to happen.

In returning to the hearing room, Joe and Terry waited anxiously hoping that they would soon know if Leo would be Salid's new lawyer. But they had a longer wait than expected, squirming in their uncomfortable seats. When Mandy did appear he said the prisoner had a request and asked that the bailiff escort her to the bench.

Shackled, with head bowed and in drab prison garb, Salid removed her veil disclosing an attractive smile and said as humbly as possible: "Your honor I wish to change my defense lawyer. I would like Mr. Leo Morrison to replace my present attorney since I feel I am not being fairly represented."

Amid the mumbling of those present, Mandy tapped his gavel once more and said in a commanding tone: "You have that right young lady. Please be advised that there will be a change in the legal representation as requested by the accused. I hereby instruct the court that Mr. Morrison will now be her defense lawyer, as she so wishes." The judge then brought things to order demanding that the next session begin and that everyone should remain seated.

As calm resumed somewhat, Terry tapped Joe on the shoulder.

"Congratulations old man! This should certainly help her. It's about time." He was suddenly interrupted, however, as he turned his head and said "But my God—look who has arrived amid all this excitement?"

"Gloria?" guessed Joe noting Johnson's surprised look. "Yeah—she's sitting in the back smiling about this…as though still on vacation," said Terry. "If she only realized she's also very much in our spotlight."

"But has our mystery woman who's following her also arrived?"

Nope—at least not yet. But she may be later on. There's some surveillance cameras hidden in the top corners of this place that'll pick Dana up if we don't."

Leo didn't let anyone down with his impressive performance once the hearing continued. He was as thorough in his presentations as he was in remaining calm and distinguished. It was clear that he had studied the case considerably and described Salid fairly—the innocent young female that was deceived by her husband in believing that the drug lord and his gang were indeed going to lead her out of her dreaded "bondage".

While this was going on, another young lady entered the courtroom—interrupting the hearing momentarily. However, it wasn't Dana, causing Joe and Terry to relax a bit. But Joe did recognize her. It was Salid's sister, Paola. She simply stopped at a row of seats in the back, and before sitting down knelt in adoration as though she was in church. Then she very gently put a handkerchief to her eyes as though wiping away some tears.

Following his premier role as a defense attorney, Leo was congratulated by Joe, Terry and the chief in front of the judge and Larson. As the room emptied out Kavinsky was bumped by Larson who, instead of apologizing, muttered with a sneer: "You bastard, I'll teach you someday not to interfere."

"What's the matter Ralph. Didn't you get your 30 pieces of gold?" Joe responded.

Salid's sister remained sitting, but hugged Salid as she was led back to the detention center. Despite weeping over this long ordeal, they both were smiling about the way the hearing was now going. It was indeed an emotional scene as Joe and Terry looked on also smiling.

Terry's smile suddenly vanished, however. "There goes Gloria, I've gotta stop her!" he almost yelled.

"But why—for gosh sake, leave well enough alone," warned Joe.

"No—now's the time to fill her in on what's going on. We've already taken too long for this anyway."

Johnson ran up to the departing Marks, already putting on her big red hat, saying: "Gloria—Let's talk. I know you're on vacation but we have to discuss a serious situation the agency wants to inform you about."

Although startled by this sudden approach of Johnson, she pointed to a place to sit down and they both began their conversation regarding her associate—but now sinister suspect—Dana Goodwin.

Instead of looking somewhat shocked by the update on Dana, Gloria simply commented, "Well, nothing really surprises me about Goodwin. She's a mean little bitch, I already knew that and I hope I never see her again."

"But we have to, soon," responded Terry. This seemed the perfect time to caution her about being followed by Dana.

Recalling an alert from the DEA, Terry warned Gloria to "check your back! watch out for Goodwin," noting the agency is sure Dana is stalking her.

"I still pack a pistol, like every good undercover person in our agency," reassured Gloria shrugging off the threat and patting her purse holding the gun.

"Yeah—and I'm sure Dana does likewise. Hopefully, she doesn't think we're on to her. She's probably still showing off her DEA credentials. Remember, we're out to catch her before she does any more killing. And, who knows, you may very well be next on her list."

Gloria took a dainty handkerchief from her pocket and wiped her forehead. "I'm a little scared about this Terry, but I'll keep my eyes open for her."

"Good—and be sure to notify us immediately if you spot her—you'll need our help. Don't try to be friendly or trust her—do you understand?"

"I sure do—I'll alert you and everyone else in the DEA office if necessary."

"Whatever it takes," said Johnson.

He added, "Oh, and by the way, I'd take that hat off—it's too much of a target. Isn't there something less conspicuous to wear?"

The color in Gloria's face almost began to match her hat when Terry said this about her favorite head-dress. It was obvious she admired it. But after blushing for a few moments, she slowly and somewhat reluctantly removed the hat and, admitting it may be too noticeable, said simply that she'd try to find something that would be more of a match for her graying hair, but indicated it may take a while to replace it.

After Gloria departed, Joe remarked, "Geez—what did the ladies all see in Dave? It sure must have been kind of nice having them fight so much over you."

"Yeah—too bad he didn't live long enough to enjoy it," quipped Johnson.

"And it also was his undoing," noted Kavinsky, thinking about his loyal and trusting beautiful wife waiting for him to come home that evening. He suddenly wanted to hug her and, of course, baby Matilda.

His thoughts were interrupted, however, when he, Terry and the chief were suddenly summoned into what they called "the hallowed chamber" of Judge Mandy.

CHAPTER 16

Mandy was standing up taking off his robe when the trio entered. He didn't say anything for at least several minutes as the visitors glanced at one another wondering that the hell was going on and, as the old cliché goes, who called this meeting anyhow? They realized usually only the defense and prosecuting attorneys were allowed.

When he did speak, his words were sharp with an edge of being threatening.

"Morrison was good, wasn't he? You fellas must be especially pleased about that. Ralph told me you set him up, he's furious. I understand this is the first time he's ever been taken off a case."

Before any response could be made, he added, "But don't congratulate yourselves too much—or too soon gentlemen. You'll recall this is also a bail hearing and if any charge is made she'll be put back into detention and await further federal determination of her fate." He added, "Also, she must pay for Leo's work."

"You don't sound very pleased about all this judge," Joe remarked.

"You're damn right I don't. We leave too many of these terrorists to our nation go free. It's a disgrace. I haven't heard enough to change my opinion."

A knock on the door interrupted the judge from continuing. It was Peter Letsen the newly announced prosecutor in the case.

"Excuse me judge. I wanted to let you know the defendant is locked up again and there is no word yet from the Attorney General's office as to what the next legal proceeding should be."

Leo also entered behind Letsen to offer some advice. "Judge, if there is now no charge the law says you have to give her a chance to at least post bail."

Mandy told Joe and Terry to leave while talking exparte with the two opposing attorneys.

"I know what the law says. It doesn't take a junior lawyer to tell me. I listened to your defense and am giving this every consideration possible in my mind," the provoked judge snapped back.

Calming down, Mandy then removed his glasses and stroked his beard as though in deep and careful thought before stating his position.

"You made her sound sweet and innocent, but not enough for me to make bail easy. Her bail should be tough, like the gang she associated with, otherwise she rightly belongs behind bars," he said.

"How tough?" quizzed Joe.

Before answering, the judge put his glasses on, sat back and looked sternly at those wondering what he was about to say next.

"Millions of dollars tough," he declared.

"How many millions," asked Joe as the others just stood there in awe of what the judge just said.

"Two million—two big ones in fact," Mandy said as though waiting for the gasp from those in his chambers.

"Isn't that sort of preposterous, judge? How and where could a little peasant girl come up with that kind of bail?" asked Kavinsky.

"Let her get that gang of billionaire Arabs to help her." was Mandy's quick response. "After all, the terrorists over in her part of the country seem to know Bin Laden and the likes, a few million is a spit in the bucket for them," he said with a shrug while moving some legal papers closer to him as though wishing to finalize this matter.

CHAPTER 17

❀

"She's certainly can't go back home—that's the last place she wants to be. The extreme Islamic group may burn her at the stake," said Leo.

"Or stone her to death," he added realizing other possibilities.

As the judge rose, indicating he wasn't about to debate his decision further, Leo interrupted: "Shouldn't you run this by the federal authorities judge—especially the U.S. Attorney's office?"

This only seemed to irritate Mandy further. "I know what I'm doing young fella. She's being charged with conspiracy and held on bail for two million dollars," he proclaimed.

As this was going on, Salid was being led once again to her dark little cell. Her sister remained with her until the cell doors were locked. She clung to Salid's hands through the bars, kissing them and wiping away her tears.

"Don't despair, dear little sister, you have friends and I'm sure you will be helped through this and will once again be free and away from harm with the grace of God."

After promising to come again tomorrow with prayer beads and a mat for Salid to kneel on and bow to the Almighty for divine assistance, Paola said farewell with a smile and further encouragement.

"Remember you are not alone—God is with you as you are with Him. We are all children of Abraham, created by one God who is looking out for all of us."

As Kavinsky and the others walked away from the courthouse, almost shaking their heads in dismay over the stiff bail, Johnson put his arm around Joe's shoulders and remarked, "Don't give up big guy, there must be a way we can fight this. The DEA has run into stubborn judges before."

"After all, we're the guilty ones," said the chief. "We all promised her forgiveness with her great help—right in my office."

With all those words still in his mind, Joe returned home rather glumly. After embracing his baby girl and hugging his wife passionately as she stirred some wonderfully scented soup for her rather defeated-looking husband, he propped his feet up on his favorite recliner and began telling Sarah the sad scenario of the day's courtroom activity.

"How long will she be held in that awful place?" asked his upset wife with her hands on her very shapely hips.

"Who knows. Leo believes she may be shipped far enough away from here to avoid any more publicity around the case and allow the judge to avoid any more embarrassing attention. He's thinking mainly about himself, of course,—he wants to come out a hero in all this. Doesn't give a damn about her."

"Where is she going to get that kind of money?...they may as well have thrown away the key to her jail," said Sarah as she began tucking Matilda into her high chair.

"Exactly—it's not like she has the money we inherited from your daddy," added Joe smiling at the struggle the baby was putting up.

Sarah suddenly stopped as the baby calmed down. "Joe what did you say?—I mean do you know what you just said?"

"Huh?" was Kavinsky's only reply wondering what his wife was so surprised about.

"We have that kind of money, Joe. After all, we received five-million-dollars from that inheritance, remember?"

"How can I forget. What are you getting at?"

"We could post her bail—we could be her savior."

"Whoa—hold up honey! There's lots of technicalities involved. And I don't even know if that would be allowed with me being part of the group attesting to her plea bargain."

"Can't you run it by your new lawyer friend Leo? He hasn't been in your group and you're impressed by his intelligence and honesty."

"He'd sure be surprised by our financial availability. Probably smack a huge fee on any advice given to me," warned Joe with a grin. "But then again, we do have some extra bucks to spare. In fact, let's also pay Leo instead of Salid doing this. I understand she's poor as a church mouse, that bastard Beck didn't leave her a cent."

After discussing the pros and cons of this situation more while trying to keep Matilda and the dog under control, they agreed that they should at least quickly check out the possibilities of helping to post bail for Salid.

There was little thought given to the risks involved in coming up with the bail until conferring with Leo. He cautioned, "If your name is on the bail, Joe, there would be lots of talk and suspicion focused on you as though you're collaborating with her."

Before Joe could respond, Leo further warned, "And there's always a possibility that she may indeed not honor her bail and flee away from all this."

Kavinsky shrugged this risk off. "No way. I trust her completely. Besides, where would she go—it certainly wouldn't be back where she came from?"

"What about your name and the controversy this might stir up among your colleagues and others who may wonder why you're interfering with Mandy's judgement?" questioned Leo.

"I'm not, he gets his bail amount—Salid goes free until, and if, charges are filed."

There was a pause as the two men pondered over this. Joe put his hand to his chin and looked down at the floor as if his intended efforts may be hopeless.

Leo was the first to break the silence by asking, "Is there any way you could post the bail with some other name?"

"Forgery? My god Leo you above all wouldn't suggest that—would you?"

"No—but perhaps there's someone in your family or your wife's who would be willing to put his or her name on the bail—using some of that inheritance you mentioned to support it."

"I only have a baby, dog and, of course, wife," Joe said frowning.

"Why not use the name of your baby or, better yet, the maiden name of your wife?" suggested Leo. "After all, they're real people and the money's under your wife's name not yours."

"Yeah—the inheritance we received was made out to Sarah Crimmons. No mention of Kavinsky. In fact, I'm sure her old man would have been mad if he knew she was marrying a cop."

"But what about the baby?"

"She's the daughter of Sarah—right? So she comes under that inheritance."

"Yeah—and Matilda is Sarah's middle name by the way."

"I'm not a contract lawyer Joe, but I'm sure you can pull this off by having Sarah Crimmons sign for this."

Before Joe could ask how much Leo was charging for such advice, now knowing his financial worth, the good-natured lawyer assured him that this was free, with the hope that the mistreated Muslim girl would be freed.

"As for all this getting misinterpreted in the news, perhaps you should also get some advice from your uncle the reporter," he further advised.

Kavinsky contacted Al quickly before even thinking about approaching the judge. He was lucky to catch Benjamin in since he knew this was about the time his uncle would be making his rounds on his news beat.

"Joe—I was just about to call you," greeted Al. "What kind of bail did Mandy set for our veiled young lady?"

"Can't tell you on the phone unc. How about you and aunt Kay dropping over to our house tonight for dinner and your favorite beer. I need some help—regarding the press. Can you make it by 8 or so…we should have the baby in her crib by then."

"Kay's going to be at her sister's, but you can count on me Joey. From the sound of things something didn't go quite right."

"You sure can smell news unc. But, hopefully, what we're going to discuss shouldn't get into print."

He no sooner clicked off when his cell phone jingled. This time it was from Terry who opened the conversation rather loudly saying: "Joe, I'm still seeing red."

Kavinsky thought he meant Terry was still quite angry over the judge's announcement of the excessive bail. But such thoughts about the apparent injustice being played out left quickly when Johnson began explaining what he saw.

"That red hat—she's still wearing that crazy thing. I saw it weaving in and out of a crowd of bystanders at our baseball opener last night. It was her—Gloria. But I couldn't spot Dana anywhere."

"We didn't want to contact her in case her stalker was nearby. But Gloria is good at using a gun, so we're not too concerned if Dana ever attacks her."

"But Dana's still packing one, too, Terry. How do you want to handle this?"

"With considerable finesse, my friend. Perhaps if we invite both to our annual DEA picnic we'll finally get Dana. Obviously, both like baseball very much. They were stars on our DEA women team. At this time, Gloria is still on vacation and I'll bet apparently enjoying much of her time off at the ballparks."

"If the crowd's yelling, perhaps their shooting won't be heard," kidded Joe. "And if Gloria's wearing that big hat, anyone sitting in back of her trying to watch the ball game may want to hit on her first."

"Don't worry, if we have them surrounded with our agents we should be able to carry this out rather smoothly," Johnson assured.

"Hopefully, none will tip them off," warned Joe.

"We'll be very close to both of them, and our team of agents is trained for such situations very carefully."

"And I'll be also there to help, if need be," offered Joe. "Just in case…"

"Thanks, but maybe you should be way back in the shadows. After all, Dana was with you when Paulson was jailed in Bermuda. She may wonder why you're around and get a little spooky and suspicious about all this."

Checking his watch, Joe changed the subject by informing Johnson about his meeting time with Al. He was careful to avoid any mention of the possibility of posting bail until this was figured out in greater detail with Sarah.

Despite the occasional bawling of the baby, the dinner with Al went well. After the usual conversation about the weather and family happenings, Joe took his uncle to the sun room to finish off their dessert. Sarah also came in after Matilda was placed back in her crib. Al couldn't help but suspect that there was an exceptionally important subject to discuss considering the serious attitude of his hosts.

Although usually very talkative, Al just listened intently, and greatly surprised, as his nephew and wife related their plans for bailing out the Muslim girl. He readily agreed to see if he could help keep his newspaper pals from blowing this up too much, noting that Mandy would certainly try to avoid any more publicity and there was no real cover up since the money indeed was in Sarah Crimmons name.

Chapter 18

"When will you let the judge know about this?" Al asked.

"The sooner the better, I sense that Mandy wants to hurry it up and keep as low-key as possible. Although federal judges are not elected, this judge was appointed for life by a conservative administration…but he knows that it pays him to be well liked by everyone, whites and blacks, Christians and Muslims…you name it."

"Yeah, but I'm sure if he isn't considered tough on anyone suspected of terrorism he would be especially criticized by those who supported him."

"That's why he wants, and needs, good press, uncle Al."

"You know yourself, Joey, I always try to be impartial in my writing. I tell it as it is—but knowing what you're saying I'll figure out an approach that won't get Salid, the judge—or you—into any hot water. And rightly so. It'll take some time to really see how this unravels without getting the public all stirred up."

"Exactly. And you might add Sarah to that list. I'm sure she'd prefer not to bring up her father's criminal past by all this."

"Only way for that would be to turn the bail money over to someone she could trust—with a name that would be completely removed from all this controversy."

"Any ideas?"

Both kept quiet for what seemed to be many minutes. Joe suddenly smiled and shook his uncle's arm as though awakening him to something remarkable.

"Why not Salid's sister? After all, she's a very holy person and one I'm very sure could be trusted in this situation."

"You mean Paola what's-her-name?"

"Yes—her Christian sister Paola Murka. I'm sure Sarah would be pleased to give her the bail money for Paola to offer it as bail to the judge. No one would know of our connection."

"And who would argue over a sister helping her sister," nodded Al totally in agreement.

"It would be considered a natural thing to do—and also provide more sympathy and realization that these two young women are inwardly good and trustworthy," added Kavinsky.

"I'll be looking forward to hearing what Sarah has to say about this. From my journalistic viewpoint, Joey, this will make excellent copy when the story's ready to be broken."

But Kavinsky also wondered what sister Paola might have to say. He knew, too, that it would be necessary to eventually let Salid know about this—if it seemed likely to happen.

Moreover, Joe felt that he should keep his distance from the bail arrangement itself. That's why he contacted Leo shortly after talking with Al. Leo certainly had a way about him that was acceptable to the judge. He was sure Leo could convince Mandy that the bail provision was legal and trustworthy, but to avoid tipping him off at this time.

After updating his wife on all these plans and getting her complete agreement, Joe attempted to get in touch with Paola. This wasn't easy since she was participating in a Christian relief program in rural Minnesota at the time. But luckily, he was able to contact her via the head of the program while she was with a class of special education children on a Christian field trip.

Surprised at hearing from the detective, the nun-like Paola seemed to quickly understand the situation and expressed her appreciation for all Joe's efforts at helping her jailed sister. She promised to return to the Twin Cities later that day to be on hand to get personally involved in this.

Kavinsky sighed in relief, thanking Paola for leaving her relief program so soon to also bring much relief to his bail plans. At the same time, Paola was making the sign of the cross, in the Catholic way of expressing thanks to God, for bringing this all together. Before ending this conversation, Joe also cautioned Paola not to mention anything to anyone about the source of the bail money she would be receiving.

Satisfied with Paola's response, Joe called Johnson on his cell phone. "Terry, I think we'll be ready to go to the judge tomorrow. My wife and I will be transferring the money needed to Salid's sister who agreed to transfer this in her name for the bail bond."

Although quite pleased about this, Johnson cautioned Joe once more regarding the importance of keeping this low-key, avoiding any connection with where the money was coming from other than from the hands of Paola.

In the meantime, the judge was sitting back in his big chair grinning, lighting up another cigar and blowing out smoke confident that his huge amount of bail could never be met. His smile faded somewhat, however, when a phone call from Johnson requested that a meeting be held the following day on the subject of the bail proceedings.

Mandy snuffed out his cigar and wondered for a moment following this call if indeed something was going on to interfere with his goal of keeping this woman behind bars. But then he quickly grinned again on thinking this would be preposterous considering no one would be able to come up that kind of money so soon, nor be willing to come to the rescue of such a controversial prisoner. At least no one he knew.

Kavinsky was exceptionally tired at the end of his work shift at the precinct mainly due to all this bail planning, but before he could even close his desk drawer another jingle from his cell phone indicated perhaps more work was heading his way.

It was Johnson again. "Joe, we got an RSVP from Gloria to our ball game, but so far haven't heard anything from Dana."

"She could be catching on," noted Joe chuckling over relating catch to baseball.

"Maybe, but the game's tomorrow. The RSVP's were supposed to be in by today."

"Well, you still have a few hours left. In the meantime I'll let you know if I hear anything about her," said Joe, anxious to get home to his little family and update Sarah on what's happening with the bail issue.

"Or see her—remember she may be among us," warmed his DEA friend.

"Can't help spotting that big red hat."

"It's what's behind that hat Joe. Remember, we believe Goodwin's stalking her and is a killer even though she's one of ours."

With that closure, Kavinsky sped home before anything else could interfere and sat down with his wife on the couch near Matilda who giggled as Stella the dog came by to lie down at their feet.

This warm and cozy scene made it quite easy for the couple to further discuss—and agree upon—secretly paying for the huge bail bond the judge was expected to demand the next morning.

Love-making took over their thoughts, however, almost immediately when they went to bed, and soon after the baby stopped crying in her crib. Their passion under the sheets almost rocked the bed as both seemed intent on clearing their minds of the disturbing matter awaiting them and letting love play its joyful role.

They were still somewhat tired from all this as the sun came up and the alarm clock alerted them that the dreaded time was approaching. Both scrutinized their bank accounts as Sarah began to make out a check to Paola Murka who, as planned, would then be advised to tuck it away in her purse and place it immediately and securely in her bank before pledging to provide the money Mandy wanted as bail for the freedom of her beloved sister, at least until possible charges and a trial are scheduled.

"Wow," was all Sarah could mutter as she wrote the many numbers needed on the check. "I sure hope this works out for all of us." Joe grinned, not able to smile much knowing the dent this could be making in their long term financial networth.

As arranged, both Joe and Sarah met with Paola at a small, out-of-the-way restaurant early the next morning, several hours before the bail signing was to take place. They made it a point to pass Sarah's check to Salid's sister in a secluded corner making sure no one else was around.

Joe instructed in his most serious voice, "Let the judge lead the conversation. He'll feel very important making his bail-requirement announcement. My uncle Al has been invited to attend so the judge will be quite dramatic in whatever he has to say. I'll give you a signal when you should present the bail money."

"What kind of signal?" asked Sarah wondering if her husband would be letting Mandy know too much about his involvement in this.

"What the heck, I'll just cough a little—or even blow my nose. How's that?"

"A simple cough will do dear," responded his teasing wife.

There was very little interruption, however, when Mandy walked into his chambers to discuss Salid's future. Everyone was quiet to hear every word out of his mouth. He was rather tight-lipped at first, looking around to see who was present.

Once he sat down and put on his specs, Mandy read over some papers from the hearing proceedings and then gazing up as if admiring the ceiling began his announcement.

"Upon reviewing my notes and the remarks of both the defense and prosecutor I must say my decision for bail was rather difficult. But in checking into the role this young lady had in this terrible terrorist attack in our own cities and state it made me realize that she was indeed an accomplice in all this and must be punished."

He held up his hand to halt any interruptions, which were apparently ready to begin by some in the room. "Let me say this: I realize a plea bargain was made—but after much thought about this I don't believe it should have ever been offered. As our Attorney General emphasized we must stop terrorism from every direction and do our part in bringing those who are involved to a quick and severe justice."

At this, the judge slammed some papers down on his desk and said firmly and loudly: "and this is why I am setting an unusually high bail for this woman who was among those threatening us and the principals we stand for.

Everyone seemed to bend forward in their chairs intent on catching the next words out of his mouth.

"The bail I have come up with should be sufficient to keep the accused away from any more of her pals who plan on terrorizing us. Frankly, if I had more of a say in this her home would forever be a jail cell."

"Or be sent back to a cell in her homeland," yelled someone in the rear of the chamber.

Kavinsky looked back at the guy yelling and wondered who he was.

"Who the hell is that?" he asked nudging his friend Leo.

"He's a lawyer. I believe from the office of Ralph Larson."

"That figures, he and Ralph must be in cahoots for a Taliban payoff."

A bailiff heard their whispering and touched his lips, indicating that Joe and Leo should shut up and let the judge continue.

"The bail I'm recommending folks is a huge one, but considering what we're confronting I would describe it as a very fair."

Avoiding any further delay for the amount to be named, and sensing the impatience running through the group, Mandy arose, clearing his voice to make his announcement, and apparently aware of a possible sensational publicity photo, even though he often tried to dodge press coverage.

Waiving his papers regarding the proceedings, the judge then proclaimed:

"The bail is for one-and-a-half million dollars."

The entire chamber became silent. All present began wondering about this surprising amount and how it could ever be acquired considering the poor background of the accused. Why was the judge making it so impossible for Salid to go free while awaiting charges that may never be filed and only possible grand jury action?

Leo broke the silence, asking the judge to reconsider based on Salid's proven help and the support she offered to authorities. "Your honor, this is not in accord with her plea bargain agreement. By rights, we have no judicial power to hold this woman any longer. After all, there are no charges yet and no grand jury has been empowered to try her."

Please, sit down Mr. Morrison. You are out of order as far as I'm concerned. I know my legal limits. She either comes up with the 1.5 million or goes back to her cell."

Meanwhile, Joe was looking all around for Paola. Sarah could hear him mumbling, "Oh my god—she's not here and we've even given her a half-million more than needed."

Mandy tapped the office bell on his desk saying: "Bailiff inform the prisoner of this decision and then remove her to an appropriate cell block for the duration of the bail bond. We hope to have a grand jury selected shortly."

Before he could continue, the chamber door was opened and a very pretty lady walked in. Joe sighed in relief. It was Paola. She smiled back at Joe while passing by to talk to the judge.

"Your honor I am here to post the bond in my sister's behalf."

Mandy sat back in his chair with his mouth opened. It was obvious that he couldn't believe what he was hearing. The bailiff tried to silence her, but the judge was required to allow her to continue:

"I am convinced of my sister's innocence and the terrible injustice being done to her despite her promised plea bargain. Because of this I am willing to pay the extreme cost of the bail."

Hearing Joe cough loudly, she then wrote out a check in front of the awed group and presented it to Mandy. "Here is the amount you asked. I would now like to take my sister with me."

Leo jumped up and spoke out again. "She has every right to do so your honor. The check is very authentic and this young lady has the money in her bank account."

Mandy reacted as though he was tricked into all this. "It will take a few days to confirm this. In the meantime, she must remain in the detention center."

"Not according to the bail agreement judge," responded Leo. "I read what was prepared over your name and it definitely states that when bail is met the accused will be set free on the grounds that she will turn up immediately when and if proceedings resume against her."

"This must be investigated further judge," shouted the representative from Larson's law firm who was now also standing up. "How could this woman come up with so much money?"

"It's her's. And it's under her name. Since when do we argue over money that's legally held by another?" responded Leo indignantly.

The judge remained quiet, as if stunned by all these unexpected happenings.

"Has her financial status been checked?" quizzed Mandy. He then looked sternly at Paola asking, "do you know the terms of this bail young lady?" Paola stared back and replied firmly, "Yes your honor. I have the money but will lose it if my sister fails to return to your court within the given time."

Shortly after the hearing concluded the two sisters hugged one another outside the temporary holding center of the federal building. Salid could hardly believe they could stroll away free, hand in hand, from all this without any police or federal escort following them.

In fact, about the only person in sight watching them gleefully heading toward Paola's car was a lady with a big red hat.

All was not gleeful and serene, however, in the Kavinsky home. "Are you absolutely positive that those two will come through for us?" asked Sarah, becoming rather disturbed.

"I know—we have our necks out. honey. But I do feel that Paola Murka is honest and reliable. I've been in this business of cops and robbers long enough to spot a phony. They both would have everything to lose and nothing to gain if they pull a fast one on us."

"But Joe, we'd be out a million-and-a-half dollars if she runs off," reminded his distraught wife.

"Nope, we're out more—two million, remember our initial check was made out for that since the judge had indicated at first that it could take a couple of million. Plus we'd be out of our faith in both of them."

"My god, how can you treat this so lightly Joe? Think of all the wonderful things that could buy for our family. And don't forget we want to pay Leo for his great effforts. I'm trying awfully hard not to have some second thoughts about how much we should trust Salid."

Realizing her concern, he gently reminded Sarah of their mutual agreement to do this, and also that they weren't exactly broke. "We still have about several million left—and I'd bet it all that we'll get it back at the right time in the right way." He said this, however, hoping Sarah didn't note the uncertainty in his voice.

Baby Matilda got them out of the funk they were in by tossing some of her ice cream to the pup. The floor was smeared, but the dog and baby seemed extremely happy knowing there was more on her high chair. Even the parents had to laugh.

There was no laughing, however, for Joe and his wife after days became weeks without hearing from Paola. They began to get more nervous every day wondering if they indeed were the ones being deceived.

Kavinsky was always comforted by calling his pal Johnson, and so, when he had the opportunity during a break in running down some dope runners, he clicked onto Terry's cell phone to find out if he had any reports on the two sisters. He knew his uncle had done his job by keeping the bail posting news very brief for the press.

"Glad you called, Joe. I haven't heard much either. I wouldn't worry about it, however, since our agent Gloria is keeping close track of the sisters."

CHAPTER 19

❦

"What's the latest on Salid and Paola?" asked Terry.

"Only that they're both enjoying some peace and quiet up north at Gull Lake. Paola has a boat and they're taking turns paddling around that scenic area."

"Sounds boring, but safe."

"Very safe, what with Gloria keeping close tabs on them. In fact, I think they're not far from your uncle's vacation cabin."

"May I ask—why Gloria?"

"Well, as you know, where she goes Dana's soon to follow."

"Why don't you just arrest Dana. Why bother to prolong this any further?"

"She seems very elusive, and we don't want a shootout. Unlike Gloria, she is still on vacation and doesn't know we think she's a suspect. Perhaps a nice trip to Minnesota's lake country is just what she's looking for—besides Gloria."

He added, "Gloria will alert us if she sees her—and we're sending some undercover guys up there to oversee all this."

"Sounds like you're watching her every step of the way, Terry. Hooray for the DEA!"

"Great slogan, Joe. "And very catchy—if you get what I mean," Johnson chuckled.

"Well, let's catch them. All I want soon is to get Paola to update me on the bail freedom being enjoyed by her sister. Also, there's a matter of half-a-million that she's still carrying around that wasn't part of the bail deal."

"I'm sure you are concerned old pal. Gloria will be keeping us well updated and you're very much in the loop. Also, if they go too far out of our area, they'll be reminded by her, as well as about honoring the demand of the court for Salid's return."

"That's quite a game of cat-and-mouse you play, Terry."

"Well, let's hope it all works, Joe, and that we'll be bringing our suspect in soon and, for your sake, those two cute Mideast girls will be showing up when requested."

Despite being somewhat reinforced by his DEA pal's words, Joe still had to face a stern-looking wife wondering what comfort and wisdom Johnson could provide.

"Don't know for sure when we'll be hearing from Paola, but the DEA is helping to keep an eye on this," Joe reported to her.

Sarah responded, "I hope they keep all of their eyes on it honey. I surely hope those women don't let us down. They looked so downhearted and sincere, you can't help but not trust them and feel sorry for what's happening."

With this in mind, Sarah slept soundly when bedtime arrived snuggled up to her husband. And from the sound of things, mostly Joe's loud snoring, neither were too worried to prevent having a good night's sleep. Even the baby slept through the night—for the very first time.

But sleepng soundly wasn't happening about 200 miles north in a log-cabin style resort so popular in the Indian countryside of Nisswa, Minnesota. It's not that Gloria Marks wasn't tired, she was—after jogging along a lake at the resort that evening, bicycling earlier in the afternoon and even playing a few rounds of golf on the resort's beautiful manicured links.

In fact, she figured she was over-tired since all this was squeezed into her assignment of keeping an eye on Salid and Paola. Both loved to exercise. Being much younger than Marks, it was difficult for the 50-year-old Gloria to keep up with them. She had to do this quite subtly since in her undercover role it was important that they didn't suspect they were being watched.

To encourage sleep, she drank some milk, took a couple of aspirin, and began reading a very boring book on rules of the DEA. She purposely put this aside when receiving it almost five years ago on becoming an agent. No one knew the difference. After all, thought Marks, she was always considered a good agent—one who contributed to the arrest of many drug smugglers and abusers since joining the agency. She was kidded by her authorities at times who liked to say that "Marks' marks were always good."

Gloria was interrupted in trying again to doze off by a slight knock—more like a tap—on her cabin door. It wasn't very late, but she wondered why anyone would want to contact her at this time. She hoped it wouldn't be the sisters she was observing. She sure didn't want to blow her cover, as the guys in the agency would say.

Slipping on a robe, she unlatched the big oak door and opened it slowly guessing whoever it was behind the door would be a maid or resort attendant with some information.

But it was neither. Instead, it was Dana Goodwin, with a big grin.

"Hi Gloria, may I come in? I have something for you," were Dana's opening remarks.

Gloria was so surprised she simply nodded, acknowledging Goodwin's unexpected presence, and before she could utter any words, noticed Dana was holding something. It was a cocked .38 revolver.

"Put that thing down, you fool! Why are you after me? I had nothing to do with your lover…he was a two-timer and you knew it."

Pushing her way into the cabin and shoving Gloria farther into the room, Dana commented, "He was cheating on me and you were the one who led him on. All the time you had me believe you hardly knew Dave and yet you were with him many times behind closed doors."

"He was cheating on everyone he could hit on. Face it Dana, Dave was a no-good scumbag who made out with everyone he could."

"But you didn't have to kill him."

Marks nearly tripped backing up from the approaching, aggressive Goodwin who began poking her with the pistol. She was speechless upon hearing this accusation and looked up at the ceiling to see if the DEA monitor was working.

While all this was happening, Terry Johnson was also observing what was happening—watching from the other end of the bugging devices planted in Gloria's cabin. However, he was a long way from quickly helping her. The camera picking up this drama was also set up in a DEA office in another resort making sure Goodwin, with all her knowledge of how the agency worked, wouldn't get suspicious.

At this point, he could only count on the ability of Marks and the fast reaction and training she received for escaping such situations. However, he realized, too, that Gloria also was trained and was considered one of the best DEA female students in coping with assault and murder intent. But he could also see the fright in Gloria's eyes as she looked back at the monitor, almost begging for someone to come rescue her.

CHAPTER 20

❀

Meanwhile, although things seemed comparatively peaceful at the Kavinsky house, inside the minds and "gut feelings" of Joe and Sarah ran thoughts of when Salid's sister would be contacting them, and would they promptly honor Judge Mandy's order for Salid to be back for charges to be announced, if that time comes.

The "if" part of that issue was still being explored. Some of the decision makers were still checking into whether Salid was ever knowingly involved in the terrorist scenario at the great Minnesota mall and clinic. Others seemed intent on calling her a terrorist and making her an example of what happens to conspirators planning to harm the nation. This was being fueled by the U.S. Attorney's office and driven by the 9/11 tragedy.

While all this was being deliberated, Joe continued on his police job investigating crime in his hometown and Sarah kept picking up after the baby who was now almost toddling. They often reminded one another that they certainly didn't need any more excitement.

However, this wasn't to be. A call from Terry added even more upset in their lives. Joe realized it was some new problem when Johnson advised him to sit down for the news he was about to tell him.

"We may have lost the sisters—they're probably still around the resort area, but our spotter Gloria hasn't reported back to us."

"You mean you've lost her, too? Maybe uncle Al could help you map this out since he's so familiar with that terrain."

"Sort of. She was tracked and attacked by Dana and somehow dropped out of sight of our surveillance cameras in Gloria's cabin. We're just afraid she might be harmed—or God knows what's happening to them. I don't think Al could help."

Following a pause, allowing Joe to think about this for a moment, Johnson added, "And Joe, a new development has come up by overseeing and hearing our monitor device that puts Gloria more in the Paulson murder scenario…perhaps even also as a suspect too. We just have to forget focusing on Salid and her sister for now until we actually know the details of the circumstances around both of our own DEA agents." Judging from Johnson's tone of voice, Kavinsky knew it was something very serious that was taking the DEA away from this matter, but realized it related mostly to authorities other than that agency and was really more of a personal concern of Joe's.

However, Terry encouraged, "We'll be sure to keep you well informed if we get any news regarding those sisters. Meanwhile Joe, I suggest you wait—and maybe pray—that Salid and her sister come through for you, and we'll do all we can to update you."

Although somewhat relieved by this, Joe couldn't concentrate much on his other police work trying to push out thoughts that the sisters fled and can't be found. He and his wife grew even more concerned when Leo Morrison informed them that the judge was on the verge of summoning a jury to soon try the case against Salid pending charges. This meant that the deadline for Salid's return was drawing very, very close.

"What if they don't show up on time, and how can they even be notified if no one knows for sure where they are?" wondered Kavinsky somewhat alarmed.

"Those are questions the court involved will have to answer, Joe. But knowing judge Mandy he will show no patience or mercy. The bail money would be forfeited, of course, and the penalties increased," noted Leo.

"In other words, they would be considered fugitives from the law?" asked Joe. "Exactly, and it would be difficult keeping your role in contributing the money for Salid's freedom a secret any longer," Leo added.

Joe admitted, "At this point, Leo, I don't know what happened to them. The last I heard they were enjoying a relaxed life on one of our lakes. My worst fear would be they were caught by the Taliban. They could be anywhere. Look at Bin Laden, he may even be in our own backyard," Joe said with a shrug.

"Yeah—and look how long Saddam was hidden until caught. Some even thought he may be here," added Leo, expanding on other not so far-out possibilities.

Trying to remain calm and positive, the detective called his uncle to obtain some more reassurance. He warned Al that he may be getting some news of the sisters fleeing and that possibly he might be involved with the story.

"Not if I can help it Joe. But if it gets picked up on the wires and network there's no way it can be stopped. The bail was clean and legal, I don't know how anyone can make a dirty issue out of it. Besides, that's very rough country up there, it would be damn hard to find anyone. I'm very familiar with that area," Al noted.

"Well, if you know of any story breaking on this—tip me off."

"Count on it nephew. But I don't see how anyone could know it—unless they had an inside track. And you and I both know that everyone involved with the bail was trustworthy and the judge certainly frowned on any notoriety or publicity regarding this case." As usual, Kavinsky felt much better after talking with his uncle. But being a detective, he always looked for motives behind any unusual activity when it came to possible crime. In checking out motives he eliminated many possibilities, one in particular, however, lingered in his mind. That was blackmail.

But who would try that? Desperation could drive anyone to anything, he learned through experience as an investigator. There's always some leverage available to encourage someone to force another to do his or her bidding, he reasoned.

However, he admitted the main reason could be if blackmailers learned he was behind posting the bail money. After all, they might think Joe would be willing to pay in many ways to keep anyone from knowing he helped set a terrorist free, or that he was so wealthy from his wife's inheritance that kidnapping the sisters could be a devious way to control how this case goes.

Other possibilities, he figured, could focus around the conniving Larson and even the suspicious looking Nakeem. He was sure Ralph would be handsomely rewarded by bringing Salid back to her vindictive, intolerant countrymen. He found it hard to characterize Nakeem, but felt that he, too, might be swayed by money and power. Plus, he couldn't rule out Gloria and Dana. Gloria was among the few who knew about the unusual bail agreement in communicating with her DEA colleagues. Indeed, she was about the only one overseeing the whereabouts of the sisters. If anyone had them within reach it would be Marks. Dana also would probably know about the bail situation from her fellow agents who, due to Johnson's strategy, remained unaware that she was a suspect in Paulson's death.

He returned to reality by realizing that both Gloria and Dana may be history, too. God only knows where they were. For that matter, both of them could be dead and buried by now if some of those who hated DEA agents ever caught them.

His thoughts also turned to what Terry mentioned about Gloria—that she may also be implicated in Paulson's murder. But how could that be?

The answer was being discussed that very moment as Goodwin still waved her pistol wildly at Marks in the lonely little cabin of the resort next to a peaceful and serene lake. "You made me do it! I warned you to stay away from him. He told me about your love affair and his plan to leave me. I couldn't let that happen Marks. And I won't let you get away with your taking my man," screamed Dana in jealous rage.

"But you took his life," Gloria responded in defense—trying to reason with her revenge-seeking, seemingly crazed attacker. "It wasn't me that did that horrible act…it was you."

CHAPTER 21

Unfortunately, Johnson missed all this exciting drama despite the surveillance bug. The camera, hidden in a corner of the cabin, for some reason blacked out shortly after Dana entered the cabin and inferred that Gloria had a part in Paulson's death. This is why Johnson told Joe that Gloria may be involved and that it would be best if his DEA office checked further into this instead of focusing so much on keeping track of Salid and Paola for Kavinsky.

"What a hell of a mess," were all the words Joe could sum up when trying to figure all this out. He recalled that Terry mentioned Dana was looking at the camera bug at first and, he theorized, apparently she spotted it and destroyed it before her mad discussion with Marks. Whatever the case, it seemed very uncertain at this time if Joe would ever see Salid and Paola again. His confidence in them was fading fast, as was his patience.

"Without anyone keeping an eye on them, we'll never know where or how to reach them when the judge summons them back," explained the detective to his concerned wife.

"Don't worry so much, honey. As you know, I'm counting on their loyalty to you."

"Yeah, and betting a ton of money on it," he reminded his trusting wife.

At about the same time, Judge Mandy was looking at his calendar and deciding on a time when he should issue his summons for Salid's return. He had to be cautions, however, since federal authorities planned to use stricter standards for identifying and detaining terrorist suspects in light of concerns about the mistreatment of hundreds of illegal immigrants following the 9/11 attack.

He was aware that the FBI and INS were themselves currently under investigation as to how they treated detainees while they were in custody. The INS reportedly failed to tell detainees within the required time why they were being held.

This all played a role in his determining the best time to bring her back to her little cell for further trial. Plus, there was the religious issue. He knew he must tred carefully in his approach to penalizing her, especially since she's a Muslim and so strongly attached to the Islamic culture.

Indeed, he was reminded by her sister, the Christian, of a reading from the Corinthians in the bible. In part it states: "There are different forms of service but the same lord; there are different workings but the same god who produces all of them in everyone." Being a churchgoer, Mandy knew this called for compassion and even forgiveness, but being a politician, which he was above all else, he didn't want to be considered "wishy-washy" on terrorism. After all, it wasn't the most popular thing to do these days.

After several more weeks of waiting to hear from either Paola or her sister, Joe grew even more restless and grabbed at every phone call in hope of hearing there may be some hope that the girl he bailed out wasn't still among the missing.

This is why he sighed in relief when he heard from Leo the lawyer who announced rather casually, "Mr. Kavinsky, I thought you'd like to know the judge has announced a deadline for the return of your Muslim lady."

Before he could ask what the date was, Leo said: "Tuesday of next week—at 9 a.m."

"What?—how could they meet this if they've gone many miles away to visit friends or can't be reached quickly? Doesn't seem fair for the judge not to grant them a little leeway," was Kavinsky's explosive response to this.

"Can't we legally do something about this to postpone it?" he asked.

Morrison could only shrug and respond, "Sorry, Joe, he has all the power. Our judicial system requires that bail time be met without any exceptions if so judged."

"Look Leo, and I'm saying this in confidence, no one knows where to reach them—not me, not even the DEA nor any of the feds."

"Ouch!—you mean they've fled? That means terrible trouble for them, and nearly everyone else involved in trusting them." Joe realized Leo was gently trying to tell him that he also would be hurt—financially as well as his reputation in being too gullible for a cop since he was so supportive of the sisters.

"What should I do, Leo? I'd like to notify them immediately," said the frustrated detective.

"You can't do anything at this point. If anyone notes your concern it will cause more negative attention than it should and even get bigger headlines in the press…despite whatever your uncle could do to suppress it," Leo explained.

Although warned to "sit tight", Kavinsky alerted Sarah in hope that they could both try to figure out some strategy to make sure bail time is met and that no panic buttons are pushed prematurely.

CHAPTER 22

❃

One person Kavinsky was sure he could confide in was his uncle. Al had again assured him that he wasn't going to let any of his newspaper pals know, and that he'd once again check the wire services and local news outlets to catch any possible reference to the sisters and try to spot them in any of the photos transmitted to his news resources…much like he did when he saw Gloria Marks' photo at the beach, with stalker Dana Goodwin in the background.

"I'd cool it Joe. I'd be really surprised if you didn't hear from them soon," Al advised. "Well, it better be damn soon. Mandy probably is already standing by wringing his hands to begin his persecution," his nephew warned.

However, at that very moment the judge was kneeling, his hands folded together prayerfully while he knelt briefly, hidden away in a corner of his chamber. He was mumbling, instead of growling, seemingly asking for divine help in his handling of the Muslim case. It was apparent he was greatly torn in two ways by wanting to please his fellow politicians, but also seeking support from God to be on his side. Praying was a side of Mandy no one knew about. He realized he had only a few true friends and the phony ones couldn't touch him since as a federal judge he received a life appointment by state senators and even the president. Although his job didn't depend on being elected, he still wanted to be well liked among his peers and sneaked in prayers to one he knew was sincere, seemingly playing "both sides" to be sure of a good outcome.

In the meantime, Kavinsky found himself pacing the floor at home while wondering when and if the sisters would show on time, or ever. He was peering at his watch as though trying to make it go slower when the phone in the kitchen rang so loudly it almost caused him to jump, as it did the baby. Matilda's crying also made it difficult for Joe to hear the caller. It was from Johnson, who sounded like he was surrounded by the jingling of slot machines.

"Joe, I'm in a casino up north, near your uncle's cabin. We nabbed Dana in a resort before she could knock off Gloria who, by the way, defended herself like a real trooper...she was always a top student in our martial arts course. Dana's admitted to everything—and is proud of it. Poor Dave, his prowling around sure messed things up," Terry mused.

He added, "But we still haven't been able to find Salid or her sister. Neither Gloria nor Dana have any clue of where they might be. Dana is almost frantic, of course, over being caught without getting her sweet revenge. You'll be surprised over who helped us nab her. I'll tell ya when I get back."

He continued, "However, Marks is still thinking straight and predicted that the sisters may be heading into the Michigan Peninsula for more sightseeing—they're both avid environmentalists, you know, having learned to love the land as little girls in the Mideast."

"Yeah—but this is a far cry from their homeland desert and torrid heat," noted Joe whose voice reflected some anxiety when he asked, "But how are we going to reach them so they know when they're due back for the judge?"

"If Gloria's right, we may have a chance by checking out the resorts and motels and hotels in the peninsula. Our DEA operatives can try this at least, as well as alert our agents in the Upper Midwest to be on the lookout for them."

"What kind of chance are we talking about?"

"Less than fifty-fifty to be honest."

"That's what I need, honesty and then some. I'm just hoping the sisters are playing it honest with me."

"Don't fret my friend. I'm almost certain they are."

"Yeah—almost," responded Joe rather unconvincingly.

With that, Kavinsky clicked off and found himself almost twiddling his thumbs nervously the rest of the day while looking at his calendar, knowing that time was approaching fast and the judge would most likely raise all kind of hell when the bonded lady fails to show up.

His upsetting thoughts were interrupted when a call came in from Leo again. "Just wanted to help you relax Joe. I understand that one of the important legal beagles won't even be at Mandy's bail termination meeting with us on Tuesday."

"Who's that?" asked Joe, expecting a big turnout at the session.

"The so-called defense attorney—none other than Ralph Larson."

"How come? He was all keyed up for this."

"Yes, I know. I understand some family emergency came up and he has to be there. Some place up in the north peninsula."

"Where?"

"In upper Michigan—it must be awfully important for Mandy to allow Ralph to be absent for this."

"Yeah—to gloat over it. But then again, if Salid doesn't show up it may be because he has her headed back to the Taliban for his reward or something. He may even be on his way to catching her right now."

"We can't be presumptive, Joe," cautioned Leo. "After all, he may have a good, well-meaning reason for being away." He added, "however, I know what you're saying. In the meantime, if I find out anything more about the upcoming session I'll be sure to let you know."

"Mum's the word, Leo, no one will ever know we've talked about this. I must say, however, that session will certainly be most interesting."

The weekend went by much too fast for the Kavinsky's. They were hoping to hear from at least one of the sisters during that time, but their phone calls and mail were scarce and gave no hint of where Salid or Paola might be. They knew one thing for certain, that the bail-release session was due to begin in only about 25 hours from the time they arose Monday after an almost sleepless night. Fortunately, Joe's day at the precinct was filled with reducing his paper work and checking out reports of criminal activities on the north side enabling him to sometimes push aside gloomy thoughts regarding the outcome of this session.

When he got home that evening his first question was whether his wife heard from either of the sisters, although realizing she would have told him so immediately upon hearing.

"I was out of the office most of the day and no messages were waiting for me to check with you, Terry or uncle Al," he explained.

"I wish I had some news for you Joe. Everything was rather quiet here—including Matilda who usually has at least one bout of screaming during the day. Even the dog didn't bark much."

"Must be they sense our concern about the missing sisters and the problem we face regarding the bond money tomorrow when the sisters are due," Joe said, trying to smile to overcome some of the tension both of them were feeling.

Even in bed while not sleeping or love making, they made sure phones and beepers were reachable. It seemed that any time there was even the slightest sound both would sit up hoping it meant someone—maybe even Salid—was trying to reach them.

"For gosh sakes, go to sleep honey," suggested Joe. "We'll both need all the rest we can get for what's happening in the morning at 9 a.m."

Rising early, Sarah and Joe made sure his aunt Kay was on hand to baby sit Matilda.

His aunt came to their house promptly and would soon be joined by husband Al who was used to sleeping in since he worked on a morning newspaper and sometimes would be covering a very late night story.

After being told of the importance for taking all calls, especially from either Salid or Paola, Kay turned to the task of caring for the baby. Before leaving, Sarah gave her the phone number to call them at the courthouse regardless of what the message might be…since it could be coming from someone holding the sisters against their will or tipping them off to where they are. Or, hopefully when—and if—they arrive for the bail hearing.

The Kavinsky's left their cell phones at home since Mandy gave his bailiff strict orders not to allow any inside his chamber, or anything that might be distracting…including TV cameras or any video or audio equipment of any kind.

Despite the rush to get to his chambers at 8:45 a.m., just before his session was to begin, the judge was still not ready. He was putting on his robe and thoughtfully rehearsing his comments on the need to hold Salid longer behind bars until the detaining process was agreed upon by the higher courts. He scoffed at the immigrant detainee procedures, considering them just more red tape to cut through to deliver justice.

Besides, he had a gut feeling that by being a little late, those in his chamber would have time to get seated and if there are any unexpected problems they could be resolved before he showed up.

After a wait of about ten minutes, making Sarah and Joe even more nervous and impatient, Mandy arrived with a stern look on his face. He glanced around, mostly to make sure no one from the media was present—especially photographers—and sat behind his big desk.

As customary with this judge, he first removed his glasses and coughed a little before uttering any words.

"Gentlemen, and ladies—of course—, as you know we're together to witness the bail termination regarding the holding of one Salid Ashid who has been accused of helping a terrorist group."

Before he continued, Leo Morrison stood up to clarify the judge's remarks. "Your honor, I must remind you that this woman has been granted a plea for amnesty by both local and federal authorities. No charges should be made, of course, unless proven beyond a reasonable doubt."

"Yes, yes—I'm getting to that counselor. Please sit down. As you all know by reading my summons, the accused has been ordered back to this chamber at exactly 9 a.m. this morning, or be subject to losing her bail money for delinquency."

Checking his watch, the judge noticed there were only ten minutes left before the end of the bail period. Looking around the chamber, he noticed Joe who was nervously peering back at the chamber door waiting for it to open for the sisters.

In a loud voice, the judge said: "Please, everyone—I must have your utmost attention. I assume everyone is ready for this to begin and I must remind you that I will not allow any commotion in my chamber. My bailiff will usher anyone out who ignores this request."

There was only soft mumbling going on when another few minutes elapsed, caused by many now realizing that the main person—Salid—hadn't arrived yet. "My god, this is nerve wracking. Where the hell are they? Sarah…we've been had," Joe whimpered almost loud enough to be heard by everyone sitting around him in the courtroom.

Before he could get any response from his squirming wife, the door of the chamber made a squeaking sound and the bailiff turned to find out who was entering.

Joe could hear his heart pumping when he looked back again at the entrance. Could it be? His question was answered upon seeing first Paola and then Salid proceeding down the hall to the front seats.

They were immediately followed by Terry Johnson, smiling and winking as he passed by Joe and Sarah. As the sisters were seated, Johnson came back to Joe and whispered, "Our DEA guys found them up north—we also had some unexpected help just in time to nab Dana—and you'll never guess who gave it to us…it was Salid."

"Boy, you sure were cutting it close," responded kavinsky wiping sweat from his forehead.

The tapping of mandy's gavel interrupted. "Gentlemen, I told you before I will not allow conversation during this proceeding."

CHAPTER 23

❀

At his command, Salid stood and bowed her head as the judge read the conditions of her bail.

"You have honored this and so the bail money will be returned, as promised. We keep our promises here," he declared as some of the attendees snickered thinking how he tried to side-step the promised plea bargain. He continued, this time with a smile, "It is my opinion that you have tried to be helpful, but that you allowed yourself to be tempted by an evil group planning terrorism within our country. I also appreciate Mr. Morrison's viewpoint that without your assistance we may not have captured this group. But the fact is, you still remained with them until you yourself were caught." He gazed around the room as though trying to determine how this was being accepted so far by the audience.

Suddenly and surprisingly Terry Johnson stood up to make a point. "With due respect your honor, something recently occurred to emphasize once more how this young lady faced danger and went out of her way to help our nation's law enforcement stop criminals."

Mandy, puzzled by this sudden outburst and not knowing what to say, nodded for him to continue. Johnson explained: "With her assistance she led us to an arrest the other day of a confessed murderer—one of our own agents unfortunately. The pursued had escaped from us, but with information offered by Salid upon our questioning of where this person might be, we were able to seize the assailant to avoid any further crime."

The judge added this to his file for amnesty, realizing that such good reports on Salid were beginning to far outweigh the alleged bad ones her initial weak defense team tried to emphasize. Besides, he thought, charges may seem unconstitutionally vague and reveal a lack of prosecutable standards, making him look bad. After all, even those DNA experts at the clinic were freed by revealing terrorists.

Mandy frowned, scratched his balding head as though in great thought and said: "Considering all this, my opinion is to release her on condition that she be placed on probation until and if an indictment is made. Any violation of this will place her once again in detainment."

"Whew"—uttered Joe as he and Sarah embraced in victory. Leo also was all smiles, knowing this case could have been transferred to a military tribunal.

"All's well that ends well," Sarah remarked as she hugged and patted her husband on the back. "Yep," agreed Joe, "And immigrant detainees no longer have to be sent back home—so thumbs down on the Taliban" he chuckled. However, he felt someone was staring at him and turned around to meet the cold eyes of the frowning disappointed Larson who apparently felt things were going his way for awhile—at least enough for him to return—but realized by the rejoicing that his evil hopes were dashed.

In his rejoicing, Joe almost didn't feel an additional tap on his shoulder. It was from Paola. She held a check in her hand, hidden in such a way that others couldn't see it. She said, "Here's one more thing you should be congratulated for Mr. Kavinsky. Your trust in us is certainly appreciated. You'll find every cent you risked on us in the check the judge has returned. In fact, we've added a tip for your wonderful support. We're sorry we haven't the means to offer more for your kindness."

Paola continued, "And, by the way, Salid will be staying and working at the convent where I reside. We can assure you that her parole will not be violated, and having a job with us will help her become a citizen and prevent deportation. Moreover, she can remain a Muslim in our Christian home. This will add to our prayers."

Joe smiled, responding, "No need for any tip. I did this without wanting any extra payback. Besides, it wouldn't be legal and I sure don't want to complicate matters." Turning to Salid Joe said, "We sort of lucked out didn't we Sal." He avoided compliments, feeling a little guilty over wondering if he would ever get the bail money back. However, he nudged his wife whispering that they should send them each a thousand or more for all their "trials" and tribulations. And he was sure Leo would be pleased with the payment they passed on to Salid to give him for his excellent legal work.

As the chamber began to empty, Salid approached Johnson and began to blush over his kind words regarding her help in catching Dana. She humbly recalled that she simply told him that she wondered who the woman was following the lady in the big red hat. She noticed her running from the resort toward a specific cabin. Johnson knew Dana had fled after losing her gun, and appreciated Salid's comments. In fact, the DEA caught their evil agent exactly where Salid indicated they would, Johnson reported.

As Joe walked out of the chamber, Salid removed the veil over her pretty face, walked over to him and kissed him firmly on the lips as Sarah looked on in wonderment—and still thinking this woman was greatly attracted to her husband.

She then knelt and put her face to the floor like Muslims in deep prayer, while her sister gazed upward to the heavens with folded hands as both, in their special and different ways, said praise to their God. After they concluded their tributes to the Almighty, Joe and Sarah said "Amen." in unison with them.

Moreover, Joe once again blushed when Salid approached him and appeared as though she was going to kiss him, but instead whispered in his ear. This time his wife, however, appeared a little uneasy knowing that this mysterious Mideast woman was rather overdoing her attention to her grinning husband.

But her suspicions were unnecessary upon hearing Salid say softly, but with great sincerity…"And thanks to our God for giving us Joe Kavinsky."

The detective, rather embarrassed by all this attention, responded, "God is God, Sally. Your God is my God. And thanks be that God was there for all of us."

And then turning to Sarah, who was both smiling and sighing in relief as she carefully tucked the check Paola gave her back into her purse, Joe added: "And please don't forget that we owe lots of special thanks to my dear and very, very generous wife."

THE END

0-595-30737-X

Printed in the United States
22478LVS00006B/63